lives *of* our *own*

lives *of* our *own*

LORRI HEWETT

DUTTON CHILDREN'S BOOKS

NEW YORK

Library of Congress Cataloging-in-Publication Data
Hewett, Lorri.
Lives of our own/by Lorri Hewett.—1st. ed.   p.   cm.
Summary: After her wealthy parents divorce, Shawna returns with her father
to the small Georgia town where he grew up, and there she experiences new
attitudes toward race relations, learns something shocking about her father's
past, and discovers a surprising link with one of the "popular" white girls
at school.
ISBN 0-525-45959-6
[1. Race relations—Fiction.   2. Interracial dating—Fiction.
3. Afro-Americans—Fiction.   4. Georgia—Fiction.   5. Schools—
Fiction.]   I. Title.
PZ7.H4487Li   1998   [Fic]—dc21   97-42984   CIP   AC

Published in the United States by Dutton Children's Books,
a member of Penguin Putnam Inc.
375 Hudson Street, New York, New York 10014
Designed by Ellen M. Lucaire
Printed in U.S.A.
First Edition
1 3 5 7 9 10 8 6 4 2

To my best girlfriends—
Bernadette, Cori, and Lyda

lives *of* our *own*

{ part*one* }

{ chapter*one* }

$\mathcal{T}$HE SOUND OF SHATTERING glass brought Shawna to her feet. One moment, she was lying on the living-room couch, staring at a television rerun—and the next, she was standing upright, facing the large front window as glass fell in a shower onto the floor. Gunshot, robbers, baseball, vandals, the possibilities tumbled through her head as she approached the window, careful to avoid the glass shards glittering on the floor. Beneath the window lay a dark, heavy-looking rock the size of a fist. A breeze lifted the sheer curtains, revealing a jagged opening.

"Lord in heaven—" Grandma Rory rushed into the living room.

Shawna's eyes caught a girl standing on the other side of the window, no more than ten feet from the house. The girl stood completely still, like she had frozen after throwing the rock.

"Hey—" At the sound of Shawna's voice, a shudder rippled through the girl's shoulders. The next thing Shawna knew, she was out the front door and chasing after her, as if she had known the girl would run.

The girl ran faster, off of the property and onto the road. Shawna had never been much of a runner and the girl had longer legs, but she got within reaching distance a few yards beyond the mailbox. She made a blind grab at the girl's sweat shirt and caught it by the hood, which made both of them lose their balance and sent them tumbling hard onto the road.

Shawna's chest rose and fell heavily. A sharp, tingling sensation in her feet reminded her that she wasn't wearing shoes. The girl turned over, her mouth twisted in pain. A few freckles stood out brightly against her pale skin. Her hair, which might have been tied up in a bun on top of her head, fell in sloppy lanks around her shoulders. Her hair looked brassy in the evening light, like it was a deep shade of red.

"I know you!" Shawna exclaimed. She was sure she had seen the girl at school; maybe they had even been in a class together last semester. But before Shawna could say anything else, the girl had sprung to her feet and was sprinting up the road.

"Is he gone?"

Grandma Rory was behind her, a shotgun held firmly in two hands.

Shawna shuddered. "Grandma—"

"It's just to scare 'em." Grandma Rory squinted, like she was trying to see farther into the deepening night. "Did you get a good look at him?"

"It was a girl. Someone from school," Shawna said, glancing at the shotgun. It was a hunting relic of her grandfather's; Shawna had never seen it outside of its case over the front door. I'm sure it's not even loaded, she told herself. But it still felt weird, seeing the gun in Grandma Rory's hands, knowing that she automatically assumed the broken window was something malicious. Shawna tried to imagine what would have happened if a window had gotten broken at Mom's house in Colorado. She pictured her mother coming out of her home office, harassed-looking. Kids, she would say.

"Let's go back in before you get yourself sick," Grandma Rory said. Shawna followed her back to the house.

Grandma Rory's house was set about a half acre off a twisting back-country road. It was long and narrow, three stories high, and surrounded on three sides by a pine forest growing endlessly around the property. The house appeared to tilt slightly to the right. Grandma Rory insisted it had been built that way. "Anyhow," she would say, "the house has been standing for a hundred years; it's likely to stand for another hundred."

The rock had left a gaping hole in the living-room window about the size of a dinner plate, with dangerous-looking spikes of glass pointing inward. Shawna couldn't get the girl's face out of her mind. The face had been instantly familiar, a face she would have seen day in and day out at Dessina High School without taking much notice. Her mind roamed up and down the rows of desks in each of her classes.

"Cori, no—" Shawna said aloud. "Kari. Kari Lang, that's who she was."

Grandma Rory stopped on the front porch, frowning. "You sure about that?"

Shawna nodded, puzzled. She could picture the girl sitting across the room from her in American history class last semester: a tall, porcelain-skinned girl with bright red hair. Shawna couldn't remember ever saying anything to her or even hearing her speak up in class. "She was in a class of mine last term. Do you know her, Grandma Rory?"

"I know some of her kin." Grandma Rory turned around to open the front door. Shawna couldn't see her face.

Shawna's eyes lingered on the broken window, then fell to the bits of glass shimmering on the ground under the porch lights. What would Kari Lang possibly have against her? Kari was just another face at Dessina High—wouldn't Shawna be the same to her?

Maybe not. She thought of the weekly column she wrote for the *Dessina Weekly Journal*: "In My Opinion." This week's headline flashed in her head: "The Old South Ball: A Tradition Gone With the Wind?" A warm flush crept up her neck as she brushed pebbles from the bottoms of her feet.

The front door opened onto the living room, where Shawna's father crawled on his hands and knees, carefully sweeping tiny shards of glass off the wood floor. He wielded the dustpan and broom awkwardly, his lanky arms and legs impeding his progress. Shawna knelt to help, but he shooed her away. "There's still glass all over the place," he said.

She made a wide arc around him to the couch. "I saw some glass outside, too."

With a wry smile, Dad watched Grandma Rory hang the shotgun in its case over the door. "How many shots you fire?"

Grandma Rory waved him off. "Oh, hush up. I just thought I'd scare the damn fool who did it, that's all."

"It was a girl," Shawna said.

"A girl?" Dad looked surprised. "Was she by herself?"

"I didn't see anyone else. I almost caught her, too." Shawna paused, feeling a sneeze coming on. When the sensation passed, she continued. "I've seen her at school."

"She says it's Allison Lang's girl that did it." Grandma Rory motioned for the dustpan and brush.

Dad sat back on his knees, wiping his hands on his pants. There was a look of instant recognition on his face. A squinting look, like he was recollecting an important detail.

"You know Kari Lang?" Shawna asked. "How do you know her?"

"I don't." Dad's lips twitched, almost like he was hiding a smile. "I know her mother."

"You know her mother—" Shawna repeated. She glanced at Grandma Rory, who kept her eyes on the floor like she was preoccupied with sweeping up the glass. But Shawna knew she was listening.

"We went to school together," Dad said. "I know she has a daughter about your age."

"But I hardly know Kari at all!" Shawna exclaimed. "We were in a class together last semester. I don't think I ever said a word to her."

Dad rubbed his chin. "She just comes up to the house, throws a rock through the window, and runs away?"

Grandma Rory motioned for Dad to get out of the way. "Go put on some shoes before you cut up your feet!"

Shawna smiled as Dad got up to do as told. It must be strange, she thought, to be a grown man living with his mother again. When her parents separated last August, her father decided to move back to his hometown in Georgia. It made sense to move into Grandma Rory's house; it was close to Dessina Junior High, where her father could teach social studies, and

Dessina High, where Shawna was now a junior, and attending public school for the first time in her life.

Across the room, last year's school picture hung on the wall in a heavy, wooden frame. In the picture she wore her uniform from Lakeview Country Day, the same blue skirt and white pilgrim-collared blouse ensemble that she had worn in some form or another since kindergarten. Looking at that picture now was like looking at another person. But you wanted something different, she told herself. That was why she was here in Dessina instead of in Denver with Mom.

Turning away from the picture, Shawna watched Grandma Rory sweep the floor quickly and efficiently, then, with the agility of someone much younger, spring to her feet to empty the dustpan. By the time Dad came back to the living room in his slippers, she was already taping wax paper over the hole in the window. What a different life Grandma Rory had from the life I'll have, Shawna thought. Shawna would never have to work hard with her hands, cook in a white lady's kitchen, take care of white children while her own children took care of themselves. It was weird to think about: Grandma Rory working hard all her life and then Shawna, two generations later, going to an exclusive private school most of her life, wondering where she would apply next fall for college. The thought made Shawna feel nervous, too. Like she had to do well in school and get accepted at a good college, be successful at whatever she chose to do. That was the only way she knew how to show Grandma Rory that she appreciated all her grandmother had gone through.

Dad joined Shawna on the couch. "So what do you think Kari Lang might have against you?"

To answer his question, Shawna got her book bag, which she had left by the front door. She took out two copies of today's issue of the school paper. She handed one to her father, the other to Grandma Rory, who had just settled into the easy chair.

Dad opened the paper straight to the editorial section and to Shawna's column. As she watched his eyes scanning the page, she went over the editorial in her head.

The Old South Ball. It was one of the first things I heard about when I moved to Dessina this year. Every spring, the week after the prom, the Civic Center is transformed into a scene from the Twelve Oaks barbecue at the Wilkes's plantation. Girls raid attics and antique dress shops for big, flouncy dresses; boys wear the gray uniforms from, as people call it here, The War of Northern Aggression. It left me with a weird feeling. It made me realize that the Old South means different things to different students at Dessina. For almost half the students, it may mean pride in the past. For the rest of us, it means a time of oppression that can't be remembered with anything but horror. But with this year's ball coming up in three weeks, I'm left to wonder, what is there to "preserve" about the Old South? . . .

Grandma Rory read slowly, paying attention to every word. Dad read quickly, so it was his face Shawna looked to first for a reaction.

"Well?" she said.

He folded the newspaper on his lap. "So you think Kari Lang was waging a sort of protest against your article?"

Shawna shrugged. Hadn't she seen Kari Lang with a clique of girls known as the Etoile Club? That was another one of the things Shawna found strange about Dessina High: this social club as exclusive as a college sorority, practically putting into law all of the snobberies of popularity Shawna always associated with public-school life. If any group would speak out against Shawna's editorial, it would be the Etoile Club.

Dad was smiling a little, even though Grandma Rory looked reproachful.

"So you were friends with Kari's mom?" Shawna asked.

"Yes, I was. We were put together to do a presentation on Shakespeare. Oh, what was that—" Dad shut his eyes and drummed his fingers on the newspaper. "Something about banishment. *The Tempest, King Lear.* I don't remember exactly."

"I guess Kari has some kind of problem with me," Shawna said. "I don't know why."

"Maybe she's jealous of you," Dad said.

Shawna almost laughed. "Jealous of me?" She had seen Kari wearing a boy's letter jacket, moving up and down the hallways with clusters of girls all dressed vaguely alike. Shawna assumed Kari had the kind of high-school life everybody hopes to have: a boyfriend, a steady group of friends. How could she possibly be jealous of me, Shawna thought, the New Girl, the one who didn't quite fit in anywhere, the one who annoyed various segments of the student body with her editorials?

"No way, she's not jealous of me," Shawna said. "She must be mad at me for putting down the Old South Ball. Well, she has a stupid way of showing it."

Deep furrows appeared on Grandma Rory's forehead. "This ball of theirs or whatever, it's been going on since who-knows-when."

"That's what I was saying in the article. Maybe it's gone on too long. Maybe it's time to end it."

"Those people have their own ways," Grandma Rory said. "If they keep their ways to themselves, why does it matter to us?"

Shawna gulped, feeling guilty. "So you're saying I shouldn't have written the article?"

"I think what your grandmother's saying is that you should choose your battles carefully," Dad said.

Shawna shook her head. "I was just giving my opinion—"

"And obviously, there are some people who have strong feelings about your opinion. What I want to know is, what are you going to do about it?"

Shawna bit her lip, not sure she understood what he was asking.

"Now this Old South Ball, what does it really mean to you?"

"I—" Shawna began, but Dad shushed her.

"Just think about it," he said.

Shawna folded her legs Indian-style and squeezed her arms over her chest, like the room had suddenly grown cold. She remembered Kari Lang looking into the front window. But Kari hadn't looked angry or mean or vindictive. If Shawna was correct, she had looked surprised more than anything else, her eyes widened and her mouth open like it was the window of her own house that had been broken. Maybe Kari Lang had something against her personally. But what? And why? It just didn't make any sense.

{ chapter *two* }

LEANING INTO THE HILL, Kari huffed and puffed as she scrambled up Old Dessina Road. Sharp, contracting little pains tingled in her legs. She ran like someone was chasing her, even though she was sure she had left everyone behind back there at the Riley house.

But something else was there with her, in the sharp breaths that knifed in and out of her lungs, in her pounding heart. Humiliation like an iron hand was squeezing her stomach. Idiot, she told herself, gritting her teeth as a draft of cold wind seared her face. It wasn't like her to do anything like that. Sweet ole Kari. Never harmed a fly.

At the top of the hill, Old Dessina Road leveled off into a modest downtown. Kari slowed to a stop, doubling over with a sideache. She knew she shouldn't have come to a complete stop like that. She knew she should walk around, wait for her heart rate to go down. She blinked, woozy-headed, then flexed her knees, listening to them pop. Darkness had settled in completely, but Kari paid no attention to it. She knew this road, every dip and curve. Maybe it wasn't completely safe to run at night; maybe some crazy stranger could be lurking behind a tree, but Kari didn't worry about things like that. Things like that never happened here. Nothing really happened here.

Once she had kneaded the ache out of her side, she stood up straight. Up ahead she could see a few discs of light: the Chevron station, a few porch lamps. A red-brick courthouse, the post office, the fire station, some old houses renovated into antique shops, some Mom-and-Pop restaurants, and that was downtown Dessina. In another hour, the whole town would be completely dark. She suddenly thought of Valentine's Day, when her boyfriend, Rick, had taken her to dinner in Atlanta. Afterward, they rode the glass elevator up to the Sundial restaurant, at the top of the Westin Peachtree Hotel. The restaurant rotated in slow circles around the city. Looking out the window at the downtown skyline, mapped out in thousands of tiny yellow lights, Kari was almost giddy. It had been like Christmas.

She wondered if she should continue forward or go back the way she came. Sometimes Kari veered off on Highway 270 and ran past the Wal-Mart, past Dessina High School, which someone must have designed with a Wal-Mart in mind. But she wouldn't run that far tonight. Instead, she stood where she was, replaying the scene at the Riley house. It was almost a matter of convincing herself it had really happened. Maybe if she hadn't stopped, maybe if she had kept running, the whole thing would have remained a crazy thought in her head, an idea.

She certainly didn't have anything on her mind when she found the stone lying on the side of the road. It was a brown shale stone the color of coffee, usually found near a riverbed, not on the street. It was as wide as the palm of her hand and heavy. Kari had put it in her pocket, even though it felt uncomfortable bouncing against her hip as she ran onto Old Dessina Road.

She had been thinking about the road. How many times had she driven up and down this road or run up and down this road? Outside town limits, Old Dessina Road became Highway 450, stretching northwest to Chattanooga and southeast to Atlanta. Her whole life, it seemed like, had taken place within about a mile of this road.

The Riley house was halfway up the hill. Kari felt herself slowing down as she approached the house. Aurora Riley used to take in her grandmother's laundry, before her grandmother moved in with Kari and her parents. Aurora Riley did laundry the old-fashioned way, with a scrubbing board and homemade starch. When Kari was little, she used to go with Ma Lila to pick up the clothes. They would wait on the front porch for Aurora to bring out the laundry. If the clothes weren't ready, Aurora sometimes brought them glasses of lemonade while they waited. Ma Lila never drank hers.

A blue Toyota Celica was parked in the driveway, SHAWNA on the license plate. Rick had noticed the car at the beginning of the year. All of a sudden, a shiny, new-looking convertible entered the student lot filled with dusty trucks, souped-up fix-em-ups, and sensible little four-doors. "Some car," Rick said, and whistled. They had both been surprised to see the small black girl emerge from the car. None of the other blacks drove anything remotely that nice. It meant Shawna had money. It was weird; Shawna, who drove a nice car and wore expensive-looking clothes, living with a grandmother who used to take in laundry.

People talked about Shawna. Everyone at school knew who she was. "Can you believe this?" Kari's friend Clare shook the newspaper angrily after reading Shawna's article about the Spring Ball. "The girl comes here from somewhere else and thinks she can start changing everything?" Kari could remember some of the article: Shawna talking about the world we live in now, how it's not "white-only" and "black-only" anymore. (That's beside the point, Rick had said.) Besides, the ball wasn't technically a school event. The Booster Club put it on every year at the Civic Center, a week after the junior–senior prom. And everybody could go to the prom. Kari knew of schools in nearby towns that still put on separate proms for black students and white students.

Shawna had written something about clinging to the past, how students at Dessina High needed to create some new traditions instead of holding on to old ones. Easy for her to say. Shawna hadn't lived in Dessina her whole life. She hadn't grown up hearing about the Spring Ball the way Kari had. Ma Lila had been crowned Belle of the Ball when she was in high school over fifty years ago. Sometimes Ma Lila's eyes would mist over as she talked about walking down the central staircase, hearing the applause, curtseying low as the crown was placed on her head, spinning around the room in the customary waltz like a bride at her wedding party.

Kari and her best friends, Clare and MC, had already ordered their dresses for this year's ball. Several weeks ago, they had driven to an antebellum dress shop in Jonesboro, supposedly the location of Tara in *Gone With the Wind*. They spent all afternoon stepping in and out of flouncy, rustling dresses. Kari imagined herself walking into the Civic Center ballroom, her hand on Rick's arm. It would be like walking into a fairy tale. And what did Shawna Riley know about that?

Kari didn't know Shawna. Not really. They had been in a class together last fall, but they sat on opposite sides of the room and they never spoke. MC had three periods with Shawna this term because she took advanced classes. MC said Shawna's mother was some kind of hot-shot lawyer in Denver and that she had taken Shawna to London and Paris over Christmas. MC had overheard Shawna talking to another girl about it in class.

Kari had been thinking about Shawna as she approached the Riley house, slowing to a stop in front of it. Out of an impulsive curiosity, she had ventured onto the property. She took a few steps, then stopped, listening for barking dogs. But all she heard was the chirping of crickets in the tall grass. She wanted to look in the window, that was all. Unseen, like a ghost. She wanted to see inside the place where Shawna lived.

But she hadn't gotten close enough to look. She cowered, about to turn away and continue on, but her hand was in her pocket and she was running her fingers over the rock's smooth surface. She pictured Shawna at school, walking through the hallways like she was ten feet tall. Shawna had a look like she was too good for this place, too big for Dessina High School. And the next thing Kari knew, the rock was in her hand and an instant later, it was smashing against the window.

For a moment, Kari had stood there, like the window was a television set and she was just watching, not really present. But then she saw Shawna's face in the broken window. Tearing her eyes away, Kari ran like no one had seen her. Panic rose in her chest as she ran faster, heard footsteps coming faster behind her. A quick jerk at her shoulder brought her to the ground, where she had fallen hard on her hip. On the ground, pebbles and dirt embedded in her legs, Kari looked at Shawna for a moment. Shawna had seemed surprised more than angry. She had a pretty face, even with her hair cut short like a boy's. A tiny, pretty face with gleaming eyes. Kari felt dumb, big and dumb, next to Shawna. Before she knew it, she was up and running, away from Shawna, away from her shame in what she had just done.

Kari hugged herself to keep from shivering. Better to just go back home, she thought. Go home, crawl into bed early, forget this night ever happened. Her legs twinged in protest as she took off running down the hill. The baggy feeling in her muscles faded as she gained her stride. It could be dangerous running this fast if a car came. But as far as she could see ahead of her, the road was completely dark. She felt gravel crunching under her feet as she lengthened her stride down the soft shoulder. The wind whipped her face as she picked up speed. This must be what flying feels like, she thought, just before takeoff.

{ chapter *three* }

SHAWNA'S ROOM TOOK UP the entire third floor. The walls sloped inward and if Shawna were taller, the room would feel much smaller than it actually was. Sitting in her window seat, looking out at the canopy of green treetops outside her window, she pictured herself in newspaper class tomorrow, pretending not to notice the snide looks of her fellow editors, Troy Frost and Kessler Menighan. Why don't you just keep your opinions to yourself? she could practically hear both of them saying. But what did either of them know, anyway? The newspaper had been just a gossip rag about the popular kids before this year. Shawna used her "In My Opinion" column to talk about issues, things that really mattered. Even Mrs. Richter thought she had good ideas for improving the newspaper.

I should call Mom, Shawna said to herself. She called her mother every couple of days, even though she rarely had much to say. It wasn't the quality of conversation that mattered, anyway. Her mother wasn't the chatty type. But every morning when Shawna opened her eyes, she imagined Mom alone in the big Tudor house. Sorry, Mom, she thought, I'm sorry I had to choose between you and Dad.

Her mother wasn't home, so Shawna tried her office. Her mother answered on the third ring. "Shawna." She spoke in what Shawna called her office voice, her words carefully enunciated, like she was speaking from a script. "How's everything going?"

"Fine—" Shawna decided not to mention the broken window.

"Are things any better at school?" Mom asked.

"School's okay."

"Everyone misses you at Lakeview. I ran into Jordan last week. He asked about you."

Shawna felt herself frowning. "What'd he have to say?"

"He wanted to know how you were doing, if you would be coming back this summer. Do you ever talk to him anymore?"

"No, not really." Shawna tried to think of a way to change the subject. "I just called to see how you were doing, to say hi."

"I miss you."

"I miss you, too." Shawna leaned against the bedpost. "Um—I have a lot of homework to do—"

"I have a lot to do, too."

"New case?"

"No, I'm just tying up some loose ends. Getting some contracts in order."

"I'll let you go, then."

"Thanks for calling."

I love you, Shawna thought. Why were those words so hard to say? Instead, she said, "I'll talk to you soon," and hung up the phone.

Jordan. Shawna flung herself onto her bed and squeezed her eyes shut. But it didn't erase his image from her mind, just as she hadn't succeeded in getting rid of his image by cutting him out of photographs. She had a shoebox full of trapezoid-shaped pictures, where she had cut Jordan out of picnics, ski trips, horseback rides, school dances. But she could still see every detail of his face behind her eyes, how his soft blond hair had fallen away from his forehead, the brown eyes that crinkled when he smiled. Shawna rubbed her eyes, her face hot under her fingers. We're just friends, they always told everybody. She had believed him when he said, "I think it'd be better if we kept this to ourselves. People might not understand."

Shawna sat up and looked at herself in the mirror. She had cut her hair short when she came to Dessina. Last year she had worn her hair to her shoulders. Last year she had stayed out of the sun. She made a face at herself. At least no one here knew about Jordan. It made her embarrassed to think of him. Besides, people didn't *do* things like that here.

Shawna heard a knocking below her, so she went down the back stairs to the door. Her room had its own entrance on the side of the house, perfect for sneaking out, if she were the type. But, she realized, she would be much more tempted to sneak out if she had more friends at Dessina High.

Shawna knew who it would be at the back door: Marlon Coleman, her closest friend in Dessina. When she was younger and would visit Dessina for two weeks each summer, she and Marlon would play in the forest behind Grandma Rory's house. Marlon was a scrawny little kid then. Seeing him again last August, Shawna's eyelids had fluttered, like she was making sure he was really there and she hadn't just conjured up some gorgeous guy in her mind. The dark skin that had earned him the nicknames Spook and Midnight when he was a little kid now looked rich and polished. He looked like a man now, over six feet tall, the years of running track and playing football displayed in his lean, muscular physique. The fluttering sensation had fallen to her chest, extending outward to her fingers and toes. Could I—it wasn't even possible to complete the thought. It would be too good to be true. Especially after the humiliation of Jordan. So far, it was friendship only. But she hadn't seen him date anyone else seriously, either.

Shawna wasn't supposed to have boys in her room, so when she saw Marlon standing at the door she took him to the back porch, where they sat on the steps. He wore jogging shorts and a T-shirt, like he had just finished running. His skin glistened with sweat. "What's going on?" he asked.

"It's been a busy night," Shawna said. "A girl threw a rock through the front window. I almost caught her, but she ran away."

Marlon didn't say anything for a moment. His forehead creased and he shook his head. "You know who it was?"

"Kari Lang. I looked her right in the face. Do you know her?"

"I know her boyfriend. He hangs out with Troy."

Shawna groaned. Troy Frost, her newspaper nemesis. Come to think of it, wasn't Kessler Menighan one of those snobby Etoile Club members, too?

"What do you think she has against you?" Marlon asked.

"I have no idea."

"You think it's your article?"

"I don't know what else it could be."

"Damn—" Marlon sighed. "I guess you just can't say anything about their ball."

"But it was so weird," Shawna said. "It wasn't like she got into a truck full of rednecks and sped away. It was just her."

"Think someone put her up to it?" From the smirk on Marlon's face, Shawna knew he was thinking about Troy and Kessler. Marlon edited the sports page for the newspaper, but he never clashed with them. Still, Shawna knew Marlon didn't like Troy and Kessler any more than she did.

"But would they do something like that?" she asked.

"Who knows?"

"And then Dad said something funny, too. He said he went to school with Kari Lang's mom. I guess they were friends."

Marlon shrugged like he didn't know what to think of it, either.

"Enough about me; what have you been up to?"

Marlon clasped his hands together. "I was down by the river. Over by the old sawmill." He inhaled deeply, like he was preparing himself to say something important.

"What's down there?"

Marlon looked evasive. "Not much."

Shawna drew her knees to her chest. "Sounds like you're up to something."

To her surprise, Marlon laughed. "I just might be."

"Really?" Shawna smiled. They might have been flirting. It was tough to tell with Marlon.

He took another deep breath. "But I don't want to say anything about it—just yet."

A girl? Shawna wondered. Maybe that's why he wouldn't say anything.

They fell quiet.

"So you going to say anything at newspaper tomorrow?" he asked. "About the window?"

"I don't know," she said. She put her head in her hands. Looking at Marlon, she wished she could just put her head on his shoulder, feel like she belonged somewhere. Wishful thinking, she thought.

"I have to go in." Her voice sounded lifeless. "I've got a lot of work to do tonight."

Marlon stood up and stretched. "All right, then. I'll see you tomorrow in class."

"See you." Shawna watched him until he disappeared around the side of the house. She could feel herself shivering even as she tightened her arms around her legs, squeezing them closer to her chest. The breeze brought a green scent of crushed grass and pine needles. She looked out over the yard at the darkened trees, wondering if she would ever be able to call this place home.

{ chapter*four* }

At the bottom of Old Dessina Road, Kari turned onto Route 14, jogging down a street of smallish frame houses, past rows of porch lights making a path to her house at the end of the cul-de-sac. Her neighborhood was nothing like Greenways, where nearly all of her friends lived and where black maids waited at the bottoms of steep driveways at the end of each day for the buses to take them over to the east side of town. Her neighborhood looked a lot like the places her friends' family maids came from: older houses on tiny, cramped lots, metal swings rusting on front porches. Most people who lived here worked in the carpet mills in nearby Dalton. Kari's father was an early-shift foreman; he left home hours before Kari woke up in the morning but was home by the time she got out of school. Kari's mother could have made enough money as a doctor for them to be able to afford a house in Greenways, but Mom seemed to prefer working in the county hospital, treating the children of poor immigrants and mill workers instead of country-club types.

"Your mother could be doing so much more," Ma Lila said sometimes when she was alone with Kari. She would whisper it, like it was a secret kept between them.

Opening the front door, Kari was surprised to see Mom and Ma Lila sitting in the parlor, which they hardly ever used. The parlor was for guests, for show, decorated with Ma Lila's antiques and china place settings. Ma Lila sat on the edge of the couch reaching toward her teacup on the coffee table. Even sitting around the house, she wore dresses and her pearl choker, like she was expecting guests. Mom sat in an armchair, a medical journal lying open in her lap. When she wasn't in her white doctor's coat, Mom lived in jeans and sweat shirts, her blonde hair pulled back into a ponytail. Kari and her mother wore the same sizes, but they rarely shared clothes. Both her mother and Ma Lila sat up as Kari walked in, like they had been waiting for her.

"Kari," Mom said in the toneless voice that told Kari she was angry.

"I'm very disappointed in you, Kari," Ma Lila said.

Kari stopped where she was. That was why they were sitting in the living room together. They had been talking about her.

"I got a call from Rory Riley," Ma Lila said. "She seems to think you threw a rock through her window tonight."

Kari said nothing.

"Of course I protested." Ma Lila picked up her teacup.

She took a delicate sip, then continued. "I couldn't imagine my granddaughter doing something like that. But Rory insisted that her own granddaughter saw you do it."

Kari glanced at Mom, who hadn't changed expression or position. She just watched gravely, so that Kari had no idea what she was thinking.

Deny it, Kari told herself, act like you don't know what Ma Lila's talking about. "I—" she faltered.

Mom leaned forward, elbows on knees. "Kari, why'd you do it?"

Kari didn't know what to say. Her cheeks felt hot. But Mom kept looking at her like she was expecting an answer.

"Do you know Mrs. Riley's granddaughter?"

Kari nodded slightly. "Shawna. She writes for the school paper. She wrote something about how she thinks the Spring Ball should be ended—"

Mom's knuckles whitened as she curled the magazine in her hands. "You're telling me you broke the Rileys' window because you disagreed with something Shawna wrote in the paper?" Her voice was low and icy.

"No!" Kari searched for words. "It was—an accident. I didn't mean to do it."

Mom said nothing, her mouth tight around the edges. Kari sucked in her breath, expecting Mom to leave the room. When Kari was little and Mom was mad at her, Mom never sent her to her room. Instead, Mom went to her own room and shut the door, saying she didn't want Kari in her sight. And Kari would stand in front of Mom's closed door, not knowing if she should knock and say she was sorry for whatever she had done. She never had the courage to knock. She always went to her room and curled up on her bed, ashamed.

She had that same horrible feeling now, watching Mom sit

silently in her anger. Like Kari was stupid. Not worthy of Mom's attention.

"I want you to go over tomorrow and apologize," Mom said finally. "And tell Mrs. Riley that you're going to pay for the window."

"How much does it cost?"

"You'll have to ask her."

"But I have Etoiles tomorrow."

"Do it before the meeting." Mom got up and went to the kitchen.

Kari watched after her, then turned to Ma Lila. Ma Lila smiled and motioned for Kari to come sit beside her, like nothing had happened.

"What's on the agenda tomorrow?" She winked at Kari. Ma Lila still went to the twice-a-year alumni luncheons with Kari, her Etoile pin shiny and polished.

"I don't know." Kari glanced toward the kitchen, where she could hear Mom putting something on the stove.

"You must be so excited about the ball." Ma Lila looked wistful. "I wish I could go with y'all when you pick up your dresses on Saturday. But you girls don't need some old lady tagging along—"

Saturday. Kari was supposed to go with MC and Clare to pick up their dresses in Jonesboro. Would Mom ground her for breaking the Rileys' window? "I can still go on Saturday, can't I?"

"Of course you can. Why couldn't you?" Ma Lila said, like she had no idea what Kari was talking about.

"I guess I have to ask Mom—"

"Now don't you go worrying about that," Ma Lila said firmly. "Your mother won't prevent you from getting your dress for the ball."

Kari nodded. Not if Ma Lila had anything to say about it, anyway.

"You just apologize to Rory Riley like your mother said and everything will be fine. And for goodness sake, will you stop slouching?"

Kari sat up straighter, thinking Mom would never say anything like that. She wondered what Mom was doing in the kitchen. Probably heating up some soup, because she was never home for dinner during the week. She was probably sitting at the table by herself, reading her medical journal, glad to be away from Kari.

Ma Lila kept chattering on about the Spring Ball, but Kari felt listless and tired.

"I've got some homework to finish up," she said. "I'm going to my room."

chapter*five*

ER LOCKER PARTNER, Sephora Jackson, didn't look surprised when Shawna told her what happened last night. "That's how those folks are," she said with a shrug.

"Those folks—" Shawna was dubious. "What do you mean?"

Sephora raised her eyebrows, like she thought Shawna had asked a really stupid question. She didn't answer. Instead, she unwrapped a sour apple Dum Dum sucker and stuck it in the corner of her mouth. The syrupy apple smell made Shawna feel slightly ill.

Shawna opened the locker and pulled out her notebooks for her first three classes.

"Kari Lang, you said?" Sephora went on. The lollipop rolled across her teeth as she spoke. "She was in my biology class last year. Never said much. I had her figured for just another stuck-up white chick. You mean her over there?" She nodded toward the entranceway, where three girls came down the hallway, heading toward the bathroom. A tall redhead walking with a slightly chubby blonde and a striking brunette. They were dressed almost alike, in miniskirts with opaque tights, short-sleeved loose tops. Cupcakes, Sephora called prim, prissy girls who wore skirts all the time. Shawna had never seen Sephora in a skirt, even though she thought Sephora's boyish figure would look terrific in the kind of pencil-slim dress she herself was too short to wear. But Sephora wore Penny Hardoway basketball shirts with T-shirts underneath, or she wore sweat shirts with jeans.

Shawna watched Kari and her friends disappear into the bathroom. From far away, Kari Lang looked like she would be a stunningly beautiful girl, her bright red hair cascading down her back and her skin pale and fragile-looking. Up closer, Shawna could see that her eyes were close-spaced and her nose dusted with freckles. She wasn't any prettier than a typical high school girl.

"You gonna say something to her?" Sephora asked.

"Of course I am."

Shawna waited for Kari to come out of the bathroom. She watched as Kari emerged alone and walked over to a bank of lockers down the hall. A tall blond boy in an orange and white letter jacket put his arms around her.

"Here goes," Shawna said and started down the hall toward Kari and her boyfriend.

Kari must have seen Shawna coming because she froze, openmouthed, like someone had suddenly beamed a spotlight on her. Kari turned away, fussing with her boyfriend's collar like she was avoiding Shawna's glare.

"It was you, wasn't it!" Shawna stopped in front of Kari. She had to look up at her to make eye contact because Kari was so much taller.

Kari turned around but she stared at the floor, not looking at her.

Kari's boyfriend put a protective arm around her shoulder. "What're you talking about?"

Shawna looked him in the face, refusing to be intimidated. "Your girlfriend put a rock through my grandmother's window last night."

Kari coughed, red-faced.

"What did I ever do to you?"

Her boyfriend looked angry. "Now look here, you can't go around accusing—"

Shawna glared at Kari. "I caught you, remember?"

Kari's blush deepened.

"If you have a problem with me, why don't you just say so?"

But it didn't look like Kari was going to say anything. Her shoulders looked stiff and tight, like she was holding her breath. She gripped a folder against her chest.

"Just stay away from me," Shawna said before walking away. Grandma Rory had called whoever it was she knew from Kari's family. From the way Kari stood there like an idiot, Shawna figured Kari probably caught hell last night. Kari looked embarrassed more than anything else, ashamed that she got caught. And her boyfriend, who looked like a total redneck, seemed as surprised as Shawna was. What a coward, Shawna thought. The least Kari could have done was stand up for herself. She remembered how Dad had said he was friends with Kari's mother when they went to Dessina High. Shawna figured Kari must be a lot different from her mother.

Shawna looked at her watch. She still had eight minutes before the second bell rang and then five minutes after that to get to newspaper class. Most days, she went straight to Mrs. Richter's classroom because there was always something to do for the newspaper. Sometimes she just wandered through the hallways, looking at people: girls wearing their boyfriends' orange-and-white letter jackets, scrawny freshman boys roughhousing with each other. Shawna remembered the nervous anticipation she had felt on her first day at Dessina High. It was an ugly place, long, flat, and brown, like a warehouse. The inside was hardly better: bright orange carpet, orange and yellow lockers. Shawna found it a little sickening, like candy corn at Halloween. But the rows of trophy cases full of mementos of state championships and county championships, pennants, and medals made the place seem exciting. Finally, I'm at a real high school, she thought. How many years had she walked through the columned entryway of Lakeview Country Day School, wearing her same uniform?

The prom posters had sprung up at the beginning of the week, advertising next weekend's dance. This year's prom had a stupid theme, "A Night to Remember," scrolled over butcher-paper posters, sprinkled with glitter. But as silly as it seemed, Shawna was still looking forward to it. Lakeview didn't have enough students to hold a real prom, so instead, there was an annual spring dance at the Cherry Creek Country Club. But from what Shawna had been told, the prom at Dessina High School wasn't a cocktail-dress-and-tuxedo function. It was basically another semiformal dance, held at the school gym on a Saturday night the week before the white students' Old South Ball.

Even if the prom would be just another semiformal dance,

Shawna wanted to be a part of it, go to Atlanta to pick out a dress, plan a romantic evening. So far, Marlon had said nothing about it. Maybe I should just come out and ask him myself, she thought.

Shawna approached the cafeteria and strained her eyes, looking for anyone she knew. She only had to look to the left, where groups of black students sat together, talking, laughing, furiously copying homework assignments, kissing. The white students were doing the same things, only on the right side of the cafeteria.

"Shawna!" Sephora waved at her from the corner of the cafeteria, where she sat on the windowsill. Marlon sat at a nearby table with a textbook opened in front of him. His eyes scanned the pages quickly, like he was trying to finish an assignment.

He looked up. "What's going on?" he said with a smile.

Shawna sat next to him. "Nothing, really. You have a test today?"

"Second period."

"Hey, Shawna." Sephora jumped down from the windowsill. "You talk to that girl yet?"

"I just did," Shawna said. "She didn't say anything at all. She just looked embarrassed."

Sitting on the windowsill by herself, Tashi Logan looked down on Shawna and the others like a queen surveying her subjects. Tashi had a long neck like Nefertiti and wore her hair in thick braids that wound crownlike on the top of her head. Shawna felt her face warming as she stopped speaking. She was acutely aware of how different she sounded from everyone else.

"Get this," Sephora turned to Tashi. "Last night, this white girl puts a rock through Shawna's window. Shawna goes running outside to see who did it and catches her. So what happened when you talked to her?"

Marlon looked up from his textbook. Tashi's comma-shaped eyebrows rose as well.

Shawna shrugged. "I just looked her in the face and asked her why she did it. She just stood there. She didn't admit it, but she didn't deny it, either."

"Must be because of your article," Sephora said. She opened another sucker and put it in her mouth. "I think it's about time somebody said something about that stupid ball of theirs." She glanced at Tashi, almost like she was looking for backup.

"I thought so, too," Tashi said.

"Thanks." Shawna felt herself smiling.

"You know what they do at that ball?" Tashi said. "They go over to Tolbert County and get all these little black kids to serve the food at the ball. Back in the day, they used to get folks from here, but we aren't having any of that anymore."

"So why don't people try to end the stupid thing, once and for all?" Shawna said. In the back of her mind, she could hear her father saying, "Choose your battles carefully." She glanced at Marlon, who wore a grave expression, like he was disturbed about something.

Sephora nodded toward the other side of the cafeteria. "You know how those folks are. They'd probably burn the place down."

Crossing her hands in her lap, Tashi leaned forward. "Youth revival starts this Saturday at New Hope. There's gonna be a picnic beforehand, and afterward I'm having a party at my house." She looked directly at Shawna. "Are you coming?"

"Um—" Shawna shifted on her heels. "I'm not a member at New Hope—"

"So?" Sephora said with her sucker in her mouth. "You can still go to the revival. It's for anyone who wants to come."

Just say yes, Shawna told herself, even though she winced at the thought of sitting through a long church service. Dad never made her go to church, even though Grandma Rory went faithfully every Sunday. "I might be busy during the day," Shawna heard herself saying. When Tashi raised her eyebrows again, Shawna added quickly, "I might have to help my dad with some stuff. I'm not sure yet. If not, I'll definitely come."

Tashi shrugged. "Suit yourself." The bell rang and she jumped down from the windowsill.

Marlon shut his book. "Ready for newspaper class?" Shawna groaned, which made Marlon laugh. "Come on, you know you like riling up the place."

"Not really," Shawna said as they walked toward Mrs. Richter's classroom. Shawna could smell a hint of his cologne. "Why don't Troy and Kessler ever get on your case?"

"Everybody likes sports."

"You have it easy."

"You know I'm always on your side," Marlon said.

It made Shawna smile to hear that.

{ chapter *six* }

KARI OPENED THE LOCKER and rummaged through the folders for her first-period notebook. Her hands shook and she could feel Rick's eyes on her back.

"You did that?" Rick asked.

Kari said nothing, staring at the orange carpet as she turned around.

He threw up his hands. "What'd you have to go and do that for?"

"Well, you know, there she is, trying to end the Spring Ball." Kari tried to make herself sound forceful. "She should keep out of it!"

Rick looked at her with his head cocked. "I dunno," he said. "It just makes you look bad."

Kari shut her eyes a moment, wishing she could erase this morning and start over. It had begun badly enough. She came downstairs for breakfast to find Mom sitting at the kitchen table, reading the newspaper.

"Don't forget about apologizing to the Rileys today," Mom had said without lifting her eyes off the front page.

"I'll do it," Kari muttered, pouring herself a bowl of cereal.

To her surprise, Mom lowered the paper as Kari sat down. "I went to school with Joe Riley," she said. "He was a friend of mine."

"You mean Shawna's dad?" Kari looked up, interested. Mom never talked much about being young.

Mom was smiling a little, but then her eyes met Kari's and the smile faded.

That's probably why she was so mad at me, Kari thought as she stirred her cereal. She had broken a window at the home of one of Mom's friends. The thought brought back that terrible feeling from yesterday as she had watched Mom leave the room, not wanting Kari to be in her sight.

On top of that, Shawna comes up to her and makes a fool of her in front of Rick. An itty-bitty thing, Rick would call Shawna. Kari felt huge standing next to her. Shawna always wore great clothes; Kari had noticed that a long time ago. Not just skirts and sweaters like the Etoiles, but designer-label outfits, the kind Kari saw in magazines.

And now Rick was staring at her, wanting an explanation. She had none to give, which made her feel worse. How could she explain what had happened when she didn't all the way understand herself?

"You mad at me?" Kari couldn't look him in the face.

Rick opened his arms and Kari snuggled into his shoulder.

She felt herself trembling as his fingertips combed through her hair. His neck was warm and smelled like Ivory soap. His lips were salty when he kissed her, like he had eaten bacon for breakfast. She glanced at a photo of them tacked up in the corner of the locker. It had been taken at her parents' mountain cabin. Kari thought they looked the same in all their pictures. Rick had a nervous little half smile that showed how much he hated getting his picture taken. Kari always wore a big smile that she thought looked kind of dumb.

"Let's go meet Troy," he said. In step, they walked down the bright orange hallway, past rows of yellow lockers. Troy's locker was in the language arts wing, near the room where he had newspaper class every morning. Troy didn't like Shawna all that much; he said she was always trying to change the way they did things in the newspaper. Kari glanced around, knowing Shawna could be coming this way any minute, but luckily, Shawna was nowhere to be seen.

Troy was sitting on the floor by his locker with a girl Kari had never seen before. She was beautiful in a way that made Kari suddenly feel plain and awkward. Even though she wore jeans and a simple tank top, the girl still managed to look like she had just stepped out of *Seventeen* magazine. She was small, with wispy blonde hair perfectly tousled around a heart-shaped face. She showed dimples when she smiled and gleaming white teeth that looked polished with Vaseline.

"What's going on?" Rick said as he and Kari sat down to join them. Kari saw his eyes immediately lock on the girl. She squeezed his hand.

"Do you know Natalie Curran?" Troy asked. "Natalie, these are my good friends Rick and Kari."

"Nice to meet you," Natalie said. Kari thought she sounded funny.

Troy eyed Natalie's shoulder, like he wanted to put his hand there. "She's new. Just transferred here after spring break."

"I'm from Columbus." Natalie laughed a little. "Ohio. I always forget that there's a Columbus, Georgia, too. But then again, I don't have a Southern accent." Both Troy and Rick were nodding attentively. Kari imagined Natalie could have been reading from a telephone book and they would still be hanging on to her every word. Natalie looked like the kind of girl who was used to boys paying attention to her.

"She turned up in my history class yesterday," Troy said.

"I spent a couple weeks in another class before I realized I was in the wrong one." Natalie leaned toward Kari. Kari could smell her perfume, but she couldn't place it. "At my old school, we learned about places like China and Africa in world history and here, the world history class is mostly about Europe. But see, I already had European history last year, so they told me I could sit in on advanced placement history for the rest of the year so I wouldn't be bored."

The first bell chimed and Natalie jumped to her feet. "I have to go. Nice meeting you." She flashed Kari a big smile, then turned to Troy. "I'll see you in class."

Troy watched her leave, his face reddened. "I'm thinking about asking her to the ball."

"All right, then!" Rick gave Troy a little punch on the arm. "Show her some of that Southern hospitality!"

Troy turned to Kari. "Hey, maybe if I ask her and she says yes, you girls can take her to Jonesboro with you this weekend."

"Um," Kari said, suddenly flattered. Maybe it would be fun to take in a new girl, introduce her to MC and Clare. Ma Lila would say pretty girls make better friends than enemies. "Yeah, I reckon so. That'd be great."

"I guess I better get in there," Troy groaned, jerking his head toward the newspaper classroom. "Who knows what Shawna Riley'll be ranting about today."

"I better get going," Kari said quickly, jumping to her feet. She didn't want to hear any more about Shawna. "I'll see y'all after first period." Rick gave her another warm, salty kiss before she left.

Kari figured Rick was telling Troy about how Shawna came up to her this morning, wanting to know why she'd broken the window at her house. She wondered if Rick thought she was stupid for doing it, even though he didn't say much about it. He didn't seem to be too mad at her. She looked back toward Rick and Troy sitting on the floor. From the back, if Kari didn't know better, it would be hard to tell one from the other. It wasn't that they looked anything alike. In her opinion, Rick was a lot cuter. Troy wore his hair buzzed so short it was hard to tell what color it was, and his face wouldn't stand out in any crowd. But Rick and Troy were built in the same way: tall, muscular, but not too stocky.

Kari knew she was lucky to be dating him. Rick and Troy were the kind of boys a lot of girls wanted to date. They were both on the baseball team and they both played football in the fall. Sometimes Kari wondered what Rick saw in her. Even if it was a good thing to be tall, Kari still thought her hands and her feet were too big, too unfeminine. She was all right looking, she thought, but not beautiful like MC, who had won the Miss Teenage Georgia pageant last year. MC had long, dark hair that lay sleek against her head, and she had a boyfriend in college. Clare was pretty, too; her thick blonde hair was her best feature. But as much as Clare tried, she couldn't lose the ten pounds she wanted to shed so that she could be slender like MC.

She figured Clare and MC wouldn't be at their locker, so she went straight to her first-period study hall. Going to the back of the room, Kari laid her head on a desk, wishing she could just forget this whole morning.

{ chapter *seven* }

*A*FTER NEWSPAPER CLASS, SHAWNA and Marlon always walked together to their second-period classes. They both took science classes: Marlon physics, Shawna chemistry. The science wing was on the other side of the building, which made for a nice long walk. Marlon seemed rather distant. He looked straight ahead as they walked through the crowd of students, not paying much attention to what was around him. A NIGHT TO REMEMBER—the glittery poster stood out against the yellow walls. You should ask him now, Shawna told herself. She looked up at him, wondering if a noisy passing period was the right time to ask him something so important.

The halls started to empty as they reached the science wing. Now or never, she thought.

"Um—" Shawna swallowed. "Prom's next week, right?"

Once it was out of her mouth, she regretted it instantly. Of course he knew prom was next week. To make up for her gaffe, she said, "I always thought people planned for prom months in advance."

"Some places, they do," Marlon said. "I guess the kids here plan months in advance for that ball of theirs."

"I guess so." Shawna adjusted the folder under her arm. "But we didn't have prom at my old school. It's a new thing for me."

Marlon nodded, still looking straight ahead.

"So do you have someone to go with? To the prom, I mean?" The words came out in a jumble. Shawna's heart pounded and she swallowed again, her throat dry.

Marlon stopped where he was and turned to her. Shawna stopped as well, looking up at his face for a reaction. He smiled a little, but his face looked guarded, like he was keeping a secret from her. Shawna sucked in her breath, then felt her chest deflate. He was going to say no.

"Hey, that's nice of you to ask, but—"

Shawna looked down at her folder, her face burning. "I just thought I'd ask." She tried to keep her voice light. She looked up, not sure if he heard her.

Marlon smiled, his eyes warm and friendly. "If I wasn't already seeing somebody, I'd love to go with you."

"Seeing somebody?" Shawna had never seen him with anyone at school.

"Yeah." Marlon's guarded look returned. "I'd like you to meet her."

"Someone here?"

He nodded, still looking secretive. "Can I come by your house later on tonight? There's something I want to talk to you about."

"Sure." Shawna made herself smile.

"You're a great girl, Shawna." Marlon backed away from her. "A great friend." He ducked into a classroom. Shawna stood there a moment, stunned. Old pal Shawna, she thought, surprised at how much that hurt.

She walked into her chemistry lab just as the bell rang. Luckily, today was a lecture day, which meant she could sit and mope to herself. Come on, it's not like prom's a big deal here, she tried to tell herself. This wouldn't be the Cinderella Prom of the paperback romances she had read in junior high. Still, she hadn't expected to be so disappointed when he said no. Shawna cupped her hands under her chin, her elbows resting on her desk. She watched students passing notes back and forth under their school folders. Across from Shawna sat Mary Catherine Woolsey; MC, everyone called her. Shawna had seen her around with Kari Lang. Keeping her head forward, Shawna looked at MC from the corner of her eye. MC was taking notes with her head down, her hair fanning over her desk. She had seemed different. Unlike a lot of the white girls, she didn't tease her hair, didn't have much of a Southern accent. Something about her reminded Shawna of her old friends at Lakeview. Shawna remembered her first day at Dessina, seeing MC in English class. She had sat next to MC and chattered away about being new in town. Shawna had expected MC to be friendly, maybe offer to introduce Shawna to some of her friends. But MC had just listened in mild surprise and, after class, left the room without saying anything. It was like someone had smacked Shawna in the face with a mirror. Just like Jordan. Look at yourself, the mirror would say. You're not one of Them.

At least in Dessina, people were honest about it, Shawna thought, turning away from MC. Not like Jordan, who pretended everything was okay between them when they were alone and acted like they were practically strangers in public. She thought of Sephora and Tashi, who went through school like the white kids weren't even there. What would they think if they knew she used to date someone white? Would they laugh and say, "I told you so," if she told them what happened? Maybe she had done something wrong by trying to be friendly with MC first. Shawna picked up her pencil and began doodling on her notebook. She felt herself frowning. She was tired of being judged by rules she didn't all the way understand. She was tired of being different.

{ chapter*eight* }

AFTER SCHOOL, KARI SLOUCHED in the back of MC's car to avoid the cigarette smoke wafting from the front seats, where MC and Clare were sharing a cigarette. MC started smoking last year, right after she won the Miss Teenage Georgia pageant. To keep trim for Miss Teenage USA, she said, but MC was already tiny and Kari couldn't see what she had to worry about. Clare smoked because MC did. Kari had tried smoking, too, but it made her feel nauseated. Mom had found the pack of Marlboro Lights in her room the day Kari bought them. "Why start a habit you know you'll have to kick later on?" Mom asked. And then she had looked at Kari like she expected an answer. Kari had none to give. She just stood there feeling like an idiot. But that had been the end of her smoking.

Watching Clare fumble as she lit another cigarette, Kari thought that Clare didn't look anything like MC when she smoked. MC held her cigarette between her first two fingers, tapping off the ash with a little flick of the wrist. MC smoked like a movie star.

Clare and MC were talking about their upcoming trip to Jonesboro this Saturday, but Kari didn't join in. All she could think about was how she would have to go back to the Riley house and apologize for breaking the window. Maybe Shawna would be there to sneer at her like she did this morning.

Kari saw MC's head tilt upward as she looked at her in the rearview mirror. "We had a debate about the ball today in English class."

Kari gulped. Had Shawna said anything about the broken window in class, making Kari look like some stupid redneck hick? "What happened?"

MC took a long drag off her cigarette and flicked the ashes out the window. "All I said was that I didn't see what all the fuss was about."

"Did anybody else say anything?"

Exhaling smoke, MC said, "Some of the kids got really into it, but I thought it was a stupid debate."

"It is a stupid debate," Clare put in. "I don't think there's anything to debate."

Kari nodded, not sure if she should be disappointed or happy that MC hadn't said anything about Shawna.

"Want to go to Taco Bell?" MC asked.

"Actually, I have to go home," Kari said. "I've gotta do something before Etoiles."

Clare turned to look at her. "What do you have to do?"

Kari hesitated. "Just—something for Mom. Can you pick me up before the meeting?"

"Sure." MC turned onto Kari's street and dropped her off in front of her house.

Daddy was home, watching TV in the den. She used to play there when she was little. She didn't have to worry about messing things up, like she did in the parlor. The carpet was dark and the couches were made of a rough plaid fabric. Kari flopped onto the couch.

"Cherry!" he exclaimed. Kari got her red hair, but luckily, not the orange eyelashes and eyebrows, from her father. "I thought you had one of those hoity-toit meetings today." He tickled her under her ribs. Kari squealed and tried to wriggle free. He scruffed her head like she was a boy.

Kari giggled and grasped at her hair. "Daddy, you're gonna mess up my hair!"

He pretended to look hurt. "So all that prissiness is rubbing off on you?"

Kari threw her arms around his neck. "You know I'm not prissy." She pressed her cheek against his. He smelled like Old Spice and carpet lint. "Can I borrow the truck now? I gotta do something. Something for Mom." She looked at him closely for any signs that Mom had said anything to him about the broken window.

He nodded. "Sure, go ahead."

Kari figured he knew nothing about it and she was glad. What would he think of her if he knew? She wished she could just sit and watch television with her father. But she had to go and face the Rileys, as much as she didn't want to.

It didn't take five minutes to drive to the Riley house. Her pulse raced as she parked on the gravel driveway. She didn't see the Toyota Celica. Hopefully that meant Shawna wasn't there.

The front window was taped up, but the hole didn't look too big. A notebook-sized sheet of wax paper covered it completely. A spider-web pattern of cracks shot out from under the paper. What would happen if she touched it? Would the whole window fall in a deluge of glass?

Kari rang the doorbell. She had no idea what she would say.

A man who looked about Mom's age opened the door. Kari thought he'd be surprised to see a white girl standing meekly at his door, but he stepped aside for her to enter, like he'd been expecting her.

The front room was bright, with pictures of family members on the walls. A large portrait of Shawna immediately caught Kari's attention. She was sitting in a garden, wearing a blue sweater and skirt that made Kari think of boarding school. There was something sophisticated about her. She was pretty in a well-cared-for, put-together way. Looking around the room, Kari saw Shawna's grandmother sitting on one of the couches. While Ma Lila wore pearls and frosted her hair white, Aurora Riley looked strong, even with the streaks of gray in her jet-black hair. Shawna had her look, but more than anything, Kari thought Shawna had her father's look. Kari glanced from Shawna's father to her grandmother, neither of whom had said a word to her so far. Shawna was nowhere to be seen. She cleared her throat.

"I came over to apologize for, um . . ." She was staring at the floor, tracing the grain of the wood with her eyes. ". . . breaking your window." She spoke in a low voice, almost under her breath. Did they even hear her?

She looked up. "I'm real sorry about it."

Shawna's father was looking at her like he felt sad for her.

He had a sweet face, she thought, a face you never wanted to see sad. All of a sudden, she wanted to cry. "Why did you do it?" His voice was gentle.

The room blurred over and Kari clenched her teeth. She lowered her eyes and shrugged, taking a deep breath to pull herself together. When she knew her voice would be steady, she said, "I'm going to pay for the window. Whatever it costs to replace it."

When Kari looked up, she saw a little smile on his face, like he was going to tease her about something. "How's your mother?"

Kari forgot her shame for a moment. "My mother?" She glanced at Aurora Riley, who frowned. But Shawna's father was still smiling, his eyes twinkling. And Mom had said something this morning about being friends with him.

"We went to school together," he said. "We're old friends."

"Um, she's fine—"

"She still working at the hospital?"

"Yes."

He looked mysterious. "Ask her if she still has the arrowhead."

"Arrowhead?"

Again, he smiled. "She'll know what I'm talking about."

"I'll tell her," Kari said, backing toward the door. "I just came by to say I'm sorry—"

"Thanks for coming by," he said. "And I'll call you with an estimate on the window."

Kari nodded, her neck feeling tight. She wondered if she would ever stop feeling embarrassed about the broken window. "Good-bye."

She left the house quickly, taking a deep breath when she got into the truck. At least Shawna wasn't there.

Kari pulled the truck out of the driveway, onto Old Dessina Road. Arrowhead, he said. It must have been some kind of secret thing between him and her mother. She wondered if Mom would tell her about it if she asked. But the thought of talking to Mom, seeing Mom's reproachful look, made her not want to go home, made her want to go someplace else. But where? Rick would be at baseball practice, but she wasn't sure if she wanted to see him right now, anyway. MC and Clare were probably at Taco Bell, hanging out there until it was time for the Etoile Club meeting. What would it be like to keep driving, shift into fifth gear and just go? Who cares where she'd end up?

But when she reached Route 14, she made the left turn as always, heading home.

chapter*nine*

$\mathcal{A}$ LITTLE AFTER SIX O'CLOCK, Kari, Clare, and MC stood at Jolie Howard's front door. Jolie lived in a plantation-style house with a second-floor verandah. Two small columns held up an arched entranceway much too grand for a small house. They were running late because Clare had spent fifteen minutes in her bathroom piling her hair in a French twist. Twice it had failed, her heavy blonde hair capsizing under the strain of bobby pins.

"Relax," MC had said. "You're already a member."

Standing in front of the door, Clare was white-faced, shifty-eyed. But two months after being chosen for Etoile Club membership, the meetings made Kari nervous, too.

Bettina opened the door and stood aside as the girls entered. She wasn't like the maids who worked for Rick's and

Clare's families, maids who had the authority to yell at and discipline the kids when they were little. Bettina was formal, called the girls "Miss," stayed quietly out of sight until needed. Kari imagined maids and butlers in stately English homes would act like that. MC said she thought Bettina was from the Caribbean somewhere. Bettina didn't work for Jolie's family. She was one of four servants who worked for the family of Kessler Menighan, vice-president of Etoiles.

The girls were ushered into an overdecorated, overfurnished living room. The room would have felt a lot bigger if nearly every bit of floor space hadn't been covered with antique chairs, heavy stuffed couches, assorted tables. Lace doilies and china knickknacks dressed the tables, reminding Kari of the homes of Ma Lila's friends. One table was set up with a tea service, with plates of tiny finger sandwiches and scones, which no one would really eat. About twenty well-dressed girls sat whispering to each other on the chairs and couches. Kari always felt herself sucking in her stomach when she walked into Jolie's house. The girls found three available chairs near the back of the room and sat down. Bettina approached them soon after, handing MC and Kari cups of Earl Grey tea, already sweetened. She motioned that she would be back soon with a cup for Clare.

Kari held the china cup and saucer in her lap, careful not to make any sudden motions that could send tea sloshing from her cup. She felt awkward and out of place, even though most of the girls were not wealthy. Only Kessler, who was coming toward them with Jolie, was truly rich. Kessler wore the kind of short, sexy dress that Kari had stared at longingly in the window of Neiman Marcus in Atlanta. She had her brown hair professionally streaked with blonde. Jolie was more formal, in a long skirt with a cardigan sweater, her chestnut brown hair cut into a short, sleek bob. Her Etoile pin, a tiny silver starburst, gleamed from her sweater. Kari had never seen Jolie in pants and had never seen Jolie with chipped nail polish or a shiny nose. She was the kind of girl who never sweated, whose face always looked like a carefully painted mask. Kari turned her hands under the saucer so that her bitten-down nails wouldn't show.

"Hi, Jolie, hi, Kessler," Clare said with an anxious smile.

Jolie and Kessler were both looking at MC. "Mary Catherine," Jolie said. No one called MC Mary Catherine but Jolie and her parents. "We need you to help us with something." MC stood up, and Kessler and Jolie led her in another direction. Clare's eyes followed MC for a moment; then she turned to accept a cup of tea and a cookie from Bettina.

"Isn't this great," she whispered.

Kari sucked in her cheeks, turned up her nose, and raised her cup to her lips. Clare stifled a giggle and Kari smiled. If I have to feel out of place, she thought, at least I don't have to feel that way alone. But, glancing around the room at the other girls, she felt the nervousness come back. Most of the Etoiles were the girls Kari had never played with growing up, who had been in their own exclusive little cliques since kindergarten. Kari was certain that the only reason she and Clare were admitted was because of MC. Having a best friend who was the reigning Miss Teenage Georgia was a big deal. MC had thought the whole thing was a hoot. She had entered the pageant on a whim and had been so calm and collected next to the pageant girls who had spent their entire lives grooming themselves to be Miss This and Miss That that she had been, as the pageant director told her, the runaway winner.

Analise Gray, a senior with Orphan Annie curls, which she always forced back into a bun, came and sat in the empty chair. She wore a white cardigan and a long skirt, like Jolie. Come to think of it, Kari realized, most of the other girls dressed either like Jolie or like Kessler. Analise leaned forward conspiratorially. "I heard they're thinking about letting that new girl into Etoiles."

"What new girl?" Kari asked.

Analise nodded off to the left, where MC, Jolie, and Kessler sat with the pretty blonde girl Kari recognized from this morning, the girl Troy was swooning over.

"Her name's Natalie Curran," Analise said. "I guess her parents got divorced and she moved here with her mother after spring break. Her mom works in one of the mills in Dalton."

Clare had a surprised look on her face. Kari must have worn the same look because Analise looked at them both and said, "I know it's weird, but she won a cover model contest in New York. *American Teen* magazine. Kessler found out about it. Can you believe it?"

Kari looked at Natalie for a moment. Beauty queen. That's what she had thought this morning. She was smiling now, but she didn't have the easy self-assurance Kari had seen that morning with Troy. She was glancing around the room, looking nervous. If Kari was right, Natalie looked like she felt out of place.

Analise left and Clare looked at Natalie. She sniffed. "I don't think she's that pretty."

"Troy wants to ask her to the ball," Kari said. "Maybe we can take her with us to Jonesboro this weekend."

Clare's eyes brightened at the thought. "Oh, yeah, that'd be something."

Kari turned again to Jolie, Kessler, Natalie, and MC. MC seemed to fit right in with them. Kari knew Kessler and Jolie were grooming MC to take over when they graduated, to be the next president of Etoiles. Kari bit her lip, suddenly worried. Would MC pull away from Kari and Clare next year? Be too good for her old friends?

Jolie made her way to the front of the room and the girls immediately hushed. "Good evening, Etoiles." Same measured voice, clipped and clear. "Will the Marshal lead us in our Etoile Pledge?"

They recited their pledge, to be forever loyal and true to the Etoiles, to never forget the bonds of sisterhood they had forged together. During the pledge, MC caught Kari's eye and winked. That made Kari smile.

After the pledge, Analise took roll. All present. Jolie started in on the business of the day.

"There are some at school who think the Spring Ball should be discontinued. You all saw the editorial in the paper on Tuesday. The Spring Ball is a tradition." Jolie's voice grew forceful. "It's been going on for decades. And furthermore, it's not an official school activity."

Kari glanced at Natalie, whose forehead was wrinkled. Kari couldn't tell if she was frowning or just thinking hard about something.

"It may be politically correct to be opposed to the ball," Jolie went on, "but to me, the ball represents everything wonderful about our past."

"Here, here!" Kessler put in.

"Tonight, I'm giving you some homework. Each member will write a letter for next week's paper. Typed. In the letter, you have to say why the ball is important to you and why it should always be continued. Kessler?"

Kessler stood and faced the club. "Bring your letters to Mrs. Richter's classroom before school tomorrow morning. I know we can't print them all, but our letters will definitely make an impact on public opinion." Kessler was the features editor for the school paper. The features section mainly covered Etoile Club events, which meant Kessler and her friends were in most of the pictures. *I wonder what Kessler thinks of Shawna,* Kari thought suddenly.

"This is a very serious matter." Jolie looked at each girl in turn. Kari thought she sounded a little threatening. "We need the full support of each club member."

Watching Jolie, Kari decided that she didn't like her all that much. She didn't like the way Jolie looked someone up and down, making a split-second decision about whether this person was worthy of her attention. *How does she do it,* Kari wondered, *make people hope she likes them even when they don't like her?*

Jolie motioned to Natalie, who stood awkwardly and looked at everyone like she knew the girls were sizing her up. Jolie took her by the arm and brought her to the front of the room.

"As you may have noticed, there's a new face here tonight," she said. "Natalie Curran. She's from Ohio, but I'm sure she will fit in well with us, and we will make her feel welcome in Dessina. I know we've finished selecting new members for the year, but I would like to make a special exception and propose her for membership."

Natalie gave a big cover-girl smile, but Kari thought she still looked out of place. Kessler got up and stood with Natalie and Jolie. Natalie stood between them, silent. Kari supposed she couldn't ask Natalie to come to Jonesboro with them now. She already had better company.

THE MEETING WAS OVER. The girls broke off into small circles to gossip and MC immediately came over to Clare and Kari to say she was ready to leave.

Ma Lila played Bingo Wednesday nights, so she wasn't home when MC dropped Kari off. Kari was glad. Otherwise, she would be grilled on the meeting. What went on? What did they talk about? And then Ma Lila would look nostalgic and talk about when she was in the Etoile Club. Sometimes she would say things like, "Your mother was such a pretty girl—" like she was disappointed that Mom never cared much for things like Etoiles and parties and gossip.

Her father was already in bed when she came in. He worked the four A.M. shift tomorrow at the carpet mill, which meant he went to bed early on Wednesday nights. Kari sat at the kitchen table and began scribbling on a notepad.

As a member of the Etoile Club, I feel that the Spring Ball— She stopped there, laying her pencil on the table. What was she supposed to say?

The front door opened and a few moments later, her mother came into the kitchen, still wearing her doctor's coat. She barely glanced at Kari as she opened the refrigerator, poured herself a glass of lemonade.

"Tough day?" Kari asked.

"Not at all." Mom joined her at the table. She reached up to unclip a barrette from her hair and shook her head, ash-blonde hair falling to her shoulders. "I set a fracture, treated a baby with an ear infection. An easy day. How did it go with the Rileys?"

Kari shrugged. "Fine. They told me they'd call and tell me how much it'd cost to fix the window. Shawna's dad asked about you."

Mom smiled with that same reminiscent look she'd had

this morning. "Joe Riley. Now that's someone I haven't spoken to in a long time."

"He said you're old friends." Kari watched Mom carefully for a reaction.

"We worked on a school project together when we were your age."

"That's it?"

If Kari was right, Mom looked a little sad. "We were very good friends. It's too bad we lost touch."

"Why did you?"

"People move away; they lose touch."

"He said something about an arrowhead."

Kari saw Mom freeze a little, just for a moment. "Arrowhead," she murmured. "Of course I still have it."

I never asked you if you did, Kari thought. "What was he talking about?"

"Oh, it was just a little something he gave me." Mom finished her lemonade and stood up.

"Sounds like something important."

"It was just a little gift from a good friend. I'm going to turn in soon. I've got an early shift at the hospital tomorrow."

"Good night." Kari watched Mom leave the kitchen; then she looked down at her letter. *As a member of the Etoile Club, I feel*— Kari drew curlicues in the corner of the page. So Mom and Shawna's dad were friends. She wondered if Shawna knew that.

Impulsively, she crumpled the paper in front of her. Anyway, she figured, what difference would one less letter make?

{ chapter *ten* }

O UR WINDOW VANDAL APOLOGIZED to us this afternoon," Dad said as Shawna came into the living room.

Shawna dropped her backpack on the floor and sank onto the couch. She had gone shopping with Sephora, who wanted to buy a new outfit for the party after the youth revival this weekend. Everything had been fine until Sephora put on a T-shirt dress that Shawna didn't think was very flattering. It hung like a burlap sack over her narrow hips. "I don't know," Shawna had said truthfully. Sephora looked at her reflection in the mirror and said, "Oh, yeah, I forget some of us don't buy clothes at Wal-Mart, right?" Shawna closed her eyes for a moment and took a deep breath. She had driven Sephora home without saying much.

"She was acting really weird when I talked to her this morning," Shawna said.

"Did she say why she did it?"

"No. She just stood there like a mouse."

Dad was grinning.

"What did you think of her?" Shawna scooted toward him, curious.

"I thought she looked a lot like her mother." He looked like he was about to start laughing. Shawna wasn't sure why.

The doorbell rang and Shawna got up to answer it.

Marlon was standing at the front door, in a T-shirt and sweat pants. The T-shirt had a gray stain down the front and clung to his chest, like he'd just come from track practice.

"I'm not used to seeing you at the front door," Shawna said.

He looked a little nervous. "I knocked at the back but nobody answered."

Shawna stepped aside. "Come in."

"Can you come out?" He sounded nervous, too. Shawna walked out onto the front porch, but he seemed to want to go farther. She followed him down the front yard to the road.

"What's going on?" she asked. The road was dark and quiet. Shawna could hear the crickets from their hiding places in the tall grass.

Marlon's dark skin was bluish in the twilight. "Someone I want you to meet."

It must be the girl he's seeing, Shawna thought. She made herself smile. "Why didn't you bring her in?"

He looked embarrassed. "Didn't know if I should or not."

"What do you—" Shawna began, but a girl stepped out from behind a tree.

She had blonde hair. That was the first thing Shawna noticed. Blonde hair pulled into a ponytail. The blonde gleamed a greenish gold in the moonlight. The hair may have been long, but Shawna wasn't sure if it was full and heavy or fine and wispy. Her eyes glittered with apprehension. They were some light color, blue or green. She was a little taller than Shawna and dressed like Marlon, in a T-shirt and shorts. They must have been running together.

"Hi," the girl said.

Shawna blinked. Why did it feel like someone had placed his hands around her neck and squeezed? She fought hard to swallow. Marlon stood next to the girl but made no move to hold her hand or touch her in any way. "Hi," she managed to choke out.

Marlon cleared his throat. "Shawna, I want you to meet Natalie. Natalie, this is Shawna."

"Hi," Natalie said again, looking as nervous as Shawna felt. What does she see when she sees me? Shawna wondered. Was she expecting Shawna to turn up her nose, look down on her?

"You wrote the editorial," Natalie said. "I liked it."

"Thanks." Shawna's voice was flat. Even sweaty, with her hair pulled up, Shawna knew Natalie was a pretty girl. Shawna imagined she had a wide, toothy smile.

"So you guys are going out?" Shawna figured she might as well say it.

They looked at the ground, as if Shawna had accused them of doing something wrong.

"Natalie's new in town," Marlon said. "Just got here over spring break."

Shawna heard a car humming in the distance and soon saw headlight beams cutting through the dark. The car passed swiftly and the humming sound disappeared into the night. "That's late in the year to move."

"Yeah," he said.

Shawna turned toward Marlon, puzzled. It was almost like they spoke different languages and Marlon stood in the middle to translate. Shawna looked Natalie in the eye. "What brought you to Dessina?"

"My parents divorced," she said. "My mom wanted to leave right away. Columbus, Ohio. That's where I'm from." She glanced at Marlon.

"Shawna came to Dessina the same way," Marlon said. "She's from Colorado."

"My mom has cousins here and we're staying with them," Natalie said. Shawna realized how strange it was to hear an accent that wasn't Southern. Natalie's words sounded rushed and a little nasal. Shawna wondered if she sounded like that. Shawna felt Natalie looking at her. Could Natalie sense how much she liked Marlon, how disappointed she was?

Natalie backed away and Shawna blinked rapidly, wondering if she had been glaring.

"I just wanted y'all to meet," Marlon said. "Maybe, because you're both new here, you'll be friends." He didn't sound all that convincing. They stood for a moment in silence.

"I have to go, or I'll be late for dinner," Natalie said to Marlon. Marlon gave a little nod and for a moment, their eyes met. Shawna felt violently intrusive. Natalie offered a little smile. "It was nice to meet you, Shawna."

"Nice to meet you," Shawna echoed.

Marlon watched her run down the road until she was out of sight. It occurred to Shawna that she had never invited them inside. Embarrassed, she wondered if Marlon noticed.

"She's very pretty," Shawna said.

"Yeah." Marlon was still looking down the road.

It was like a puncture in her side. "Um—how did you meet her?"

They walked toward the porch. "Out," Marlon said. "She lives off Route 12. If I go by the river I run right by her house." Shawna sat on the porch swing and Marlon sat on the floor, facing her. "She lives out by that old sawmill."

Shawna knew what he was talking about. Last fall, when the leaves were turning colors, she and Marlon had walked along the river about ten miles. Just outside of Dessina was a sawmill that had been shut down years ago. It was abandoned, the doors rusted shut. By the mill, the river was red and sludgy, like it was still polluted by mill dust. Not far from the mill were a few blocks of run-down-looking houses. Mostly immigrants lived out there now, Dad told her, people from Vietnam and Cambodia who worked in the carpet mills. Once they had walked past the sawmill and past the houses, they crested a steep hill. At the top, they stood looking down into a valley of forests, streaked with red and gold. Shawna remembered feeling Marlon beside her, his fingers inches from hers. If he kisses me here, I'll die, she thought. He had looked at her, his face gentle, and he had squeezed her hand in his for a moment. But he hadn't kissed her.

"You here?" Marlon asked.

She shook her head. "What?"

"Looked like you were far away."

"It's nothing," Shawna said. Did he take Natalie up there? she wondered.

"I'd seen her at school," Marlon said. "And one day I was running by and she was sitting on her porch crying. I didn't know her, so I figured there was nothing I could say, so I kept going. But on my way back, she called out to me. She asked me to come up on the porch, but I told her to come down to the street. She ended up walking me halfway back to my house."

"Did you find out what was wrong with her?"

"I guess her dad doesn't send money and things are real tight. She got in a fight with her mom. Next day at school, she hung out after track practice and we started talking and stuff. I guess I'm her only friend here. And one night, we were out walking, and—"

"But you've been keeping it quiet."

"So far. But she doesn't want to be quiet about it. When you wrote that article, it really did something to her. She really got mad about the Old South Ball thing. And I guess those Etoiles or whoever tried to get her to join up with them tonight and that made her even angrier. She doesn't think we should hide things."

"What do you think?"

Marlon shrugged. "I don't like sneaking around any more than she does, but I don't know. Anyhow." He reached into his pocket and pulled out a crumpled sheet of paper. "We—did something. I don't know it it's the right thing to do. I wanted to ask you."

"Ask me what?" Shawna felt herself stiffen.

He handed her the crumpled sheet of paper, warm from his skin. "We worked on it today. We thought maybe you could sneak it into the newspaper before it goes out Monday night."

Shawna unfolded the paper. **THE OLD SOUTH BALL IN BLACK AND WHITE**, by Natalie Curran and Marlon Coleman. Scanning the words quickly, her eyes bulged. "You really want to do this?"

"It's what she wants," Marlon said. "She doesn't see why the two of us couldn't go to the Old South Ball together."

"But do you want to go?"

"Maybe you're right and the whole Old South Ball thing is wrong. I don't know," Marlon said. "I just hate going behind people's backs. It's like we have to be ashamed about being together, and we're not."

"Oh, Marlon—" Shawna squeezed her eyes shut, her heart thumping in her chest.

"Can you do it?" he asked.

She nodded slightly and Marlon smiled, the same gentle smile he had when she thought he would kiss her. I guess I am just a friend to him, she thought.

"See you tomorrow," he said.

Choosing your battles. Shawna thought of what Dad had said. She stared at the paper in her hand and it blurred over. She swallowed hard until the feeling went away. So Natalie was worth it to him. Obviously, she had no fear of being seen in a small Southern town with a black boy. Natalie looked like a homecoming queen, the kind of girl any white boy in town would be proud to have on his arm. Why did she have to pick Marlon? Shawna hated her, just a little.

{ chapter *eleven* }

SHAWNA DROVE TO SCHOOL the next morning with the top down, letting the cold morning wind wake her up. The convertible was a sixteenth-birthday present; Mom gave it to her right after she and Dad split up. Shawna always assumed it was a guilt present. At Lakeview, many of her classmates drove nicer cars than she did. But the first day she drove to Dessina High, she noticed that her car was one of the nicest, and the newest, in the student lot. It meant she stood out to the other students. People looked at her suspiciously. Simple jealousy, Mom would say. But it made Shawna wish sometimes that she drove something less conspicuous.

She couldn't stop thinking about last night, about Marlon and Natalie. C'mon, be a good sport, she tried to tell herself as she parked in the student lot. If they really liked each other, what did it matter? Wasn't that what she had thought with Jordan? But that was the problem. She hadn't thought about it at all with Jordan. It didn't even occur to her that there *could* be a problem until Jordan made her think so.

But Marlon was different. He didn't want to hide his relationship with Natalie. They wanted to see each other out in the open. Shawna had an editorial in her backpack to prove it. But was it right, to bring their relationship out in public like this? Especially at Dessina High?

All I know is that Natalie better not be just fooling around with Marlon, Shawna thought as she quickened her step down the hallway. She tried not to look at the prom posters lining the walls. A NIGHT TO REMEMBER. Not this year, anyway.

Troy Frost and Kessler Menighan were already in Mrs. Richter's classroom when Shawna arrived. The two of them were huddled together, looking through a pile of papers. Shawna set her backpack on a chair and went to join the conference. "Letters," Kessler said as Shawna pulled a chair up to the table. "These came in yesterday. All in support of the ball."

Shawna picked up a letter. "So I'll read through them and pick some to print this week."

"We were thinking we should all decide together," Troy said.

Shawna glanced at him, then returned her attention to the letter in front of her. *I'm writing to completely disagree with last week's editorial about the Spring Ball—* Jolie Howard, Analise Gray, Clare Dennington; Shawna recognized the names. "These letters are all from the Etoile Club," Shawna said.

"Yeah, we all wrote." Kessler tossed her blonde-streaked hair. "We all feel strongly about this. We're not gonna let somebody tell us what we should and should not do."

"I thought we were talking about picking which letters to print," Shawna said, sitting up a little higher in her chair. She could play snob, too. "I'll go through the letters with my staff like always and we'll pick the ones to print."

"But you're biased—" Kessler began, then fell quiet as Mrs. Richter entered the room.

"How can you kids spar so early in the morning?" Mrs. Richter said, bringing a breeze of cold air with her. Mrs. Richter was one of those teachers Shawna knew at first glance she would like. She was in her early thirties, wore Indian print skirts and little round glasses, but for all her ex-hippie looks, she kept herself discreetly out of all school controversies.

"We got a lot of letters to the editor about Shawna's article," Troy said. "We're trying to figure out which ones to print."

Mrs. Richter shrugged as she took off her coat. "Isn't that the job of the editorial staff?"

"Well, yes, but because the editor might be biased, we thought all the editors should have a say," Troy said, watching Mrs. Richter for a response. If they agreed on anything, it was that they all liked and respected Mrs. Richter.

"Why don't we give the editorial staff the chance to do its job?" Mrs. Richter said, and Troy clamped his mouth shut in sullen acceptance. Shawna could hear her father's voice in the midst of her annoyance. Pick your battles carefully. Walk away from trivial things. So Shawna did just that. She crossed the room to sit at an empty desk and pulled out her notes for this week's column. After all, Shawna thought, we still have a newspaper to put together, Old South Ball or no Old South Ball.

Marlon was running late. Shawna tapped her pencil impatiently as more of the staff began to file in. Troy and Kessler were still huddled together, going through the letters. Shawna bit the end of her pencil. It did look like there were many more letters than usual. Lisa Jaenke, another Etoile snob, brought in a large envelope full of letters.

"These were in the in-box," she said, giving Shawna a cool look. And, as Lisa sat with Troy and Kessler to look through the letters, Shawna could tell by their expressions that most, if not all, of the letters were pro–Old South Ball, anti-Shawna. It's your job to pick the letters for the editorial page, Shawna told herself. Go over there and take them. But she didn't move. She knew she shouldn't be intimidated. Mrs. Richter would back her up.

Marlon came in as the bell rang. He took the desk next to her and glanced over at the little conference across the room. "What's going on with them?"

"I guess a bunch of people wrote letters to the editor about the Old South Ball," Shawna said under her breath. Marlon looked at Troy and Kessler, then back at Shawna. Yeah, it's gonna be one of those days, he seemed to tell her with his eyes. Shawna smiled back, grateful for an ally. Then she stood and marched over to Troy, Kessler, and Lisa.

"There are almost a hundred letters here," Troy said. "What if we did an extra page insert?"

"I'll take these now," Shawna interrupted. The three of them stared at her openmouthed as she gathered up all of the letters and took them off the desk. As Kessler readied herself to protest, Mrs. Richter broke in.

"It's obvious we have a controversy on our hands here," she said. "How are we going to show both sides of this issue?"

"What's the controversy?" Troy argued. "This isn't even a school event!"

Mrs. Richter took a deep breath, as if she were taking in all of the tension in the room and diffusing it. "Whether the

Spring Ball is an official event or not, it still affects this school, and there are bound to be strong feelings about it on both sides. Personally, I think Shawna's editorial was very effective."

Kessler's and Troy's mouths fell open, and Shawna tried to hide her smile.

"It brought an important issue out in the open," Mrs. Richter continued. "And it gave students something to respond to. Instead of arguing over which letters to put on the editorial page, what if we presented two contrasting op-ed pieces?"

"Like a point /counterpoint?" Shawna asked.

"Exactly. Now I'm expecting Shawna will take the con position—" Mrs. Richter began.

"I'll write the pro," Troy said.

And that's where I take things over, Shawna told herself. I can substitute Marlon and Natalie's article for this whole pro/con Old South Ball business. The idea made her feel a little queasy. She looked at Marlon, who was poring over some photographs with his sports staffers. She hoped he knew what he was getting himself into.

{ chapter *twelve* }

BOTH MOM AND MA LILA were at the kitchen table when Kari came downstairs for breakfast Friday morning. Ma Lila was making pancakes.

"Y'all are up early," she said, sitting at the table. Mom wore a navy blue suit, her hair in a French twist. When did her mother ever wear makeup? But Mom looked elegant and sophisticated dressed up.

"I'm going to a seminar this morning in Chattanooga," Mom said.

"How many pancakes?" Ma Lila asked from the stove.

"Two, please," Kari said.

Ma Lila brought the pancakes to the table. "By the way, when does Mary Catherine give up her crown?"

"First of June." Kari poured syrup on her plate.

"What a lovely experience. Justine Jaenke said her grand-daughter Lisa's going to compete in Miss Georgia Peach next month. You're friends with Lisa, right? Etoile sisters?"

Kari half shrugged and half nodded. Lisa was just another girl in the club who probably wouldn't speak to Kari if it weren't for Etoiles.

"When Justine got the entry form, I asked her to get one for you," Ma Lila said. "It's on my dresser."

Mom raised her eyebrows. "You want to be in a pageant, Kari?"

Kari put her fork down, her face hot. It sounded like Mom was making fun of her. "I don't know—"

"It's a lovely pageant. You can win a scholarship, a trip to Jekyll Island," Ma Lila said.

Mom was smiling when she stood up. "I don't want to be late. Have a good day." She left the kitchen and Kari scowled at her plate. She hated when Ma Lila talked about pageants around Mom.

"So what do you think, Kari?" Ma Lila looked eager. "We'll go down to Atlanta and buy you a lovely dress—"

"I don't know," Kari said. She remembered helping MC get ready for Miss Teenage Georgia last year, standing back as MC held out her arms and twirled in her silver-white gown. Kari had watched MC up on the stage as the crown was placed on her head. What would that be like, she wondered, everyone looking at you, thinking you're beautiful, clapping for you? But then she had looked at the other girls, the smiles pasted on their faces as they clapped for MC. I'd probably just be one of them, standing in the background, Kari thought.

"Wouldn't it be fun?" Ma Lila said.

Kari sighed. "I don't think so."

She heard a horn blaring outside. "That's MC," she said.

"Thanks for breakfast." Picking up her book bag, she went outside and hopped into the backseat of MC's car. MC's eyes were covered with dark sunglasses and her hair looked tousled and windblown. Why can't I be more like MC? Kari thought.

"Guess what!" Clare turned around, excited-looking. "Major news. Troy asked Natalie to the ball and she said no!"

"How do you know?" Kari asked.

"Analise saw Natalie at the A&P last night and she asked her if she was going to the ball with Troy. And Natalie said Troy asked her but she said no. Can you believe it?"

"Maybe she has a boyfriend back home," MC said.

"But even if she does, she could have gone with Troy as friends or something," Clare argued. "I don't get why she wouldn't want to go to the ball."

"Want to hear a rumor?" MC said with a Mona Lisa smile. Kari and Clare leaned toward her because MC didn't spread rumors very often.

"Kessler called me late last night," she said. "She saw Natalie last night with Marlon Coleman."

Clare frowned. "You mean the—track guy?"

Marlon Coleman. He was the kind of guy everyone at school knew of. He played football in the fall and ran track in the spring and was always written up in the newspapers. Rick talked about him sometimes. So did Troy, because Marlon did the sports page for the newspaper. Rick and Troy seemed to like Marlon. He was the kind of boy that everyone liked, but Kari wasn't sure she knew anyone who really knew him.

"She was driving down Old Dessina Road and she saw them running together, about seven last night," MC said. "Kessler said she thought they looked pretty cozy."

"How can people look cozy when they're running?" Clare asked.

"I think he's good-looking," MC said.

"MC!" Clare's eyes widened. She bit her lip. "So you think—Marlon and Natalie?"

"Maybe they're friends or something," MC said.

They were quiet the rest of the ride to school, but Kari imagined they were all thinking the same thing. Every now and then, they heard a rumor about some girl dating a black guy, but it was always the same kind of girl: a girl with a reputation for being wild. The kind of girl Rick and Troy would call a slut. And after a girl had that kind of rumor spread about her, then she had to go on dating black boys, because white boys wouldn't date her anymore.

"But why?" Clare blurted suddenly.

"There might not be anything to it," MC said.

"But she's gotta know that people are gonna wonder," Clare said.

"Maybe it's different where she's from." MC pulled into the student parking lot.

They didn't say anything more about it as they went into the building. Instead of going to the bathroom, Kari went straight to Rick's locker. Rick and Troy were sitting against the row of lockers, glum-looking.

"Hey, Troy." Kari looked at Rick, who shook his head slightly.

"Hey," Troy muttered. "Know any girls looking for a date to the Spring Ball?"

"Oh, come on, any girl'd be happy to go with you," Kari said.

Troy looked embarrassed. "Not any girl."

"I'm sorry about Natalie," Kari said.

He shrugged. "I'm not the first guy to get turned down for a date."

"I don't get it," Rick said. "I thought she really liked you."

"Is she going with someone else?" Kari asked.

"She didn't say." Troy stood up. "I gotta get back to newspaper. Catch y'all later."

"It's too bad," Rick said, watching him leave. He kissed the top of her head. "At least I don't have to worry about who I'm gonna take to the ball."

Kari smiled. "Of course not." As they kissed, the first bell sounded.

Kari groaned as she thought of sitting in study hall all first hour. She didn't have any homework to do. She got a library pass from the teacher and went to the library instead. Sometimes, when she had nothing to do, she would pore over the atlases, making lists of places in the world she wanted to visit.

Kari drifted down the aisle toward the old yearbooks, going back to the 1930s. Kari pulled 1969, 1970, 1971, and 1972 off the shelf and brought them to the table. It was fun to look at old yearbooks. Mom didn't keep things like that around the house. Clutter, she called it. All that stuff was in the attic somewhere.

Opening 1969, Kari turned the pages slowly. Same building, but even in black and white, everything looked newer, shinier. She turned the pages until she reached the freshman students, near the back. Kari scanned the pages until she found Mom's picture. At fourteen, her mother had a pinched, birdlike face, almost hidden by a shaggy haircut. Her smile was timid. In the 1970 book, Allison Craighead looked more self-assured; her hair was long and straight. By 1971 she was beautiful. She wore an Indian print shirt and her hair lay straight against her head like MC's. Her smile was calm. The picture stood out from the other pictures on the page, like her mom had been different. Of course she was, Kari thought. She didn't care about things like Etoiles and she was friends with Joe Riley.

Kari turned the 1969 book a few pages until she got to Joe Riley. He had a wide, anxious-looking smile and a large Afro. Kari imagined him being awkward and skinny. But just like her mother, by 1971, Joe Riley was handsome, wearing the same calm, pleasant expression he wore when Kari went to the Riley house to apologize for the window. Maybe that year, they both figured out who they really were. In the picture, Joe Riley looked confident, like he wouldn't let petty things bother him. They met in their junior year; that's what Mom had told her. Kari flipped through the yearbook, but she never saw them in a picture together. There was something odd about the pictures. It wasn't until she got to the sports section and saw some black and white students standing side by side in football uniforms that she noticed almost every school club was segregated by race. Sixteen white cheerleaders smiled at the camera, fifty white Future Homemakers of America. There was a white glee club and a black gospel choir. It was like two separate worlds in the same school.

Kari opened 1972 and browsed through the senior pictures. Crabbe, Craddock, Crawford, Crayburn—no Craighead. Kari looked again. No picture of her mother anywhere in the senior section. She checked the index but saw no listing for Allison Craighead. Out of curiosity, she turned to Riley. She saw a Steve Riley, a white boy with acne who wrote that he wanted to be an Air Force general. But no Joe Riley. At the end of the senior section, she checked the "Not Pictured" list for both Allison Craighead and Joe Riley. Both names seemed to have vanished from Dessina High's collective memory.

Kari slammed the book shut loudly enough to get an admonishing look from the librarian. Was it a coincidence? Had her mother ever said anything about her senior year of high school? Any time she did talk about high school, it was just that: "When I was in high school," no specific reference to any year. She'd seen the diploma; it hung in Mom's office along with her diplomas from the University of Georgia and the University of Georgia School of Medicine. So why wasn't she in the yearbook or even mentioned in "Not Listed"? And why wasn't Joe Riley in the yearbook?

Instead of meeting Rick during passing period, Kari went straight to the newspaper room, where she knew she would find Shawna. Kari paced impatiently outside the classroom until Shawna emerged. Shawna was about to walk right by her; she looked preoccupied with something. Kari said "Hey!" and Shawna stopped and looked around.

"Shawna," Kari said, suddenly nervous.

"What?" Shawna looked impatient. Kari faltered. What if she was just wasting Shawna's time?

"There's something we should talk about," Kari said. "About our parents."

Shawna looked interested.

"I don't have much time right now—"

"What lunch period do you have?" Shawna cut in.

"Uh, first."

"Me, too. We'll talk then." She turned around, like she was about to walk away.

Kari felt stupid. "Where? I mean, where do we meet?"

"How about here?" Shawna said. "See you later."

Kari watched Shawna hurry off, disappearing into the crowd of students. She's kind of rude, Kari thought. No, she corrected herself, businesslike. She was the type of person who could just take charge of things. It was exciting, having something between them like this. It was like having a secret.

{ chapter *thirteen* }

HAT COULD KARI LANG possibly want to talk about? Shawna wondered as she sat through her next two class periods. Something about their parents, she said. So she must have known their parents were friends when they were in high school. But it didn't exactly mean that she and Kari suddenly had something in common.

"Bryan Clay asked me to prom this morning," Sephora said when Shawna met her at their locker during passing period.

Shawna made herself smile. "That's great."

"Eddie's coming up from Morehouse so we're gonna double with Eddie and Tashi. When's Marlon gonna get around to asking you, anyway?"

Shawna shrugged as she rummaged through her locker.

She didn't feel like talking about it. "By the way, guess who I'm having lunch with today?"

Sephora crossed her arms and leaned against the locker. "I'm not gonna guess so why don't you just tell me?"

"Kari Lang. She wants to talk about our parents."

"Your parents?"

"My dad and her mom were friends when they were in high school." Shawna shut the locker. "I don't know what she wants to talk about."

"That's kinda funny," Sephora said as they made their way down the hallway.

"Is that supposed to make us friends, too?"

Sephora laughed. "Who knows? Tell me about it."

KARI WAS WAITING FOR her outside of Mrs. Richter's classroom after third period. She stood off to the side, timid-looking, as Shawna came out. For a moment the two of them just looked at each other. Two pink spots rose on Kari's cheeks and she gave a little smile. Shawna returned it.

Kari glanced toward the classroom door as MC Woolsey came out of the room. "MC," she said, "can you tell Rick I'll see him later on? I'm gonna stay here for lunch today."

MC nodded. She looked at Shawna without saying anything and Shawna felt herself stiffen. She was getting ready to give MC a snobby look in return, but MC's look wasn't snobby, like Shawna expected it to be. In fact, MC looked surprised. She gave Kari a little smile and walked away.

"I like your clothes," Kari said, still blushing.

"Thanks." Shawna was taken aback. She glanced down at her wide-legged pants, leather clogs. Nothing spectacular there. Maybe Kari was just being polite. "It's nice to be able to wear normal clothes."

"What do you mean?"

"I had to wear uniforms at my old school."

Kari wriggled her shoulders and stared at the floor. "I guess I wouldn't like that much." Kari looked down at her feet a lot when she spoke, Shawna noticed. It made her sound like she wasn't sure of herself.

"It saves having to pick out something to wear in the morning."

Kari nodded and smiled a little.

It didn't seem like Kari was going to just come out with whatever she had to say, so Shawna decided to take the lead. "I didn't bring anything for lunch."

"Me neither."

Shawna looked at her watch. "We have enough time to get something."

"Where should we go?" Kari followed after her.

"I don't care," Shawna said. "Where do you usually go?"

"Taco Bell," Kari said. "What about you, where do you go?"

"Depends," Shawna said as they left the building. "How about the Oldtown Deli? They have good sandwiches."

On their way to the car, Shawna saw Kessler and some of her clique standing by the flagpole. They were looking at Kari, or at Kari with Shawna, in a way that made Shawna smile. She wondered if Kari noticed.

"My car's up ahead," Shawna said. With her keys, she flipped the automatic lock. Once they got to the car, she pressed a button and the top folded down.

Kari settled in the front seat and looked around the car. "This is really nice."

"It was a birthday present."

"Um—" Kari began. "I was looking through the yearbooks this morning. Old ones. I was looking at pictures of my mom, and then I noticed something funny."

Shawna kept her eyes on the road. "What?"

"My mom was missing from the senior yearbook. So was your dad."

"Missing?"

"They weren't there. You know how sometimes people are sick on picture day, and they get put in a list that says 'Not Pictured'? Well, they weren't there, either."

"Hmm." Shawna didn't know what to say.

"You think it was a coincidence?"

Shawna saw the deli up ahead and pulled into the parking lot. When she parked the car, she looked at Kari. "Do you?"

Kari seemed startled, like Shawna had just asked her a trick question. "Um—"

"I have no idea what it means," Shawna said.

"I've seen my mom's diploma," Kari said. "I know she graduated from Dessina. What about your dad?"

Had she ever seen her father's diploma? She couldn't remember having ever seen it. But you haven't seen his college diploma either, she told herself; it's not like Dad displays the stuff. Of course he graduated from Dessina; where else would he have graduated from? "I've never been told otherwise," she said. "But I've never seen his diploma or anything. Or any pictures."

"I haven't seen any pictures, either," Kari said. "I was thinking about it all morning. I've seen pictures of Mom at college graduation and med school graduation, but nothing I can remember from Dessina."

Shawna thought for a moment.

"Does your dad ever talk about high school?"

"Not much," Shawna said. "Stories and stuff. General stuff."

"I was trying to think if Mom ever talked about her senior year. She talked about being in class with your dad, but that was when they were juniors. What do you think it means?"

"I don't know." Shawna glanced at her watch. "But we'd better hurry if we want to get back to school in time."

THEY SAT EATING THEIR sandwiches in the car. Neither of them said anything for a few uncomfortable minutes.

"Do you miss where you come from?" Kari asked.

"Sometimes."

Kari nodded again, like she wasn't sure what to say. "You're from Colorado, right?"

"Denver. Well, the suburbs."

"Must be real different."

"Yeah." All of a sudden, Shawna felt sad. She stared at the dashboard as an ache gnawed at her insides. It wasn't home-sickness—not quite. Shawna wasn't sure what it was.

"I've never been out west," Kari said.

"It's really pretty. The mountains, I mean. But there are mountains here, too." She turned the ignition. "I'm going to ask my dad about his senior year."

"I'll ask my mom."

They were quiet as Shawna drove them back to school and parked in the student lot. They said good-bye and went off in separate directions. In spite of everything, Shawna thought, Kari seemed like a nice girl. A little weird, maybe, but nice. Shawna wondered what she was really trying to say. Did she mean that something was possibly going on between Dad and her mother? That would be a bold thing to admit to, especially in Dessina. Shawna didn't know what to think of it.

{ chapter*fourteen* }

RICK WAS WAITING FOR Kari outside her classroom after fourth period. "MC says you went out to lunch with Shawna Riley."

"Yeah."

He looked puzzled. "What do y'all have to talk about?"

Kari shrugged. She usually told Rick, MC, and Clare everything. But this she wanted to keep to herself.

Rick put an arm around her shoulder. "So what's up?"

"Nothing." She shrugged his arm off her shoulder.

Rick stopped walking and put his hands on her hips. "You're not gonna tell me what's going on?"

Kari felt herself growing angry. "So you're saying me and Shawna can't be friends?" But she was embarrassed as she said that. She didn't think Shawna saw her as a friend.

"Considering you threw a rock through her window, I don't see what y'all have to be friends about."

When would she ever live that down? Kari crossed her arms over her chest. "We just talked, that's all. Is that okay with you? Or do I have to get permission from you when I wanna talk to someone!"

Rick blinked and Kari immediately felt bad. "Forget it." He started to walk away.

"Rick, wait—" Kari caught up with him. He was walking with his head fixed straight ahead, not looking at her. He didn't put his arm around her shoulder.

"I didn't mean for us to get into a fight."

Rick didn't turn around. "I didn't know we had anything to fight about."

"We don't," Kari said.

Rick nodded, tight-mouthed, then went into his classroom without saying anything else. Kari stood there a moment. Why am I acting so weird all of a sudden? she thought as she turned away. She meandered down the hall. The bell was about to ring any minute.

"Kari!" Clare rushed down the hall toward her. "I'm gonna be late."

"Me, too," Kari said.

Clare squeezed her folders to her chest. "I was just talking to Analise and she said that Jolie and Kessler are going to Jonesboro on Saturday, too. And she thought maybe we could all meet downtown in Atlanta, and—"

"What?"

Clare was looking at her closely. "Did you hear anything I just said?"

"Oh." Kari shook her head, distracted. "Yeah. Saturday."

"Is something wrong?"

"No." Kari took a deep breath. "I—just had a little tiff with Rick, that's all."

Clare looked sympathetic. "I'm sure it's nothing."

"You're right."

The bell rang and Clare's eyes widened. "Gotta run. See you after class!" Clare darted into a classroom.

Kari went into her science classroom. Luckily, the teacher was facing the blackboard, so Kari snuck to her seat. During class, she couldn't think about ions and chemical reactions. None of that stuff made any sense, anyway. Instead, she thought about Shawna and what she had found this morning in the yearbooks. She couldn't wait to get home and ask her mother about it.

Mom wasn't back from the conference, so when Kari came home from school, it was just her and Ma Lila. Kari figured she wouldn't be able to talk to Mom until late Saturday, when she got home from Jonesboro. Ma Lila was watching a black-and-white movie on TV. "I'm going to keep the Miss Georgia Peach entry form on my dresser," she said.

"I don't think I want to be in a pageant." Kari sat next to Ma Lila on the couch.

"You girls must be so excited about tomorrow," Ma Lila said.

"Yeah," Kari said. She had described her dress to the last detail to Ma Lila, several times. And she had to admit, it would be fun to try it on with Ma Lila Sunday morning. Ma Lila would show her how to sit and stand gracefully while she wore so much skirt.

"I was looking through my trunk earlier for my white gloves," Ma Lila said. "And you can wear my baroque pearl necklace, too."

"Thanks." Kari had seen black-and-white pictures of Ma

Lila as the Belle of the Ball, wearing long white gloves. Kari had tried them on before. They itched, but they made her hands look smaller.

"Ma Lila—" Kari thought of how she should broach the subject. "At school today, I was looking through Mom's old yearbooks and, well, I didn't see Mom's senior picture."

Ma Lila sipped her Coke without a change in expression.

"Was Mom absent on picture day?"

"No, it wasn't that." Ma Lila folded her hands in her lap. "I know I've told you."

"Told me what?"

"I mean, it's no secret. Your mother got sick. She took a trip to Gulf Shores in June and I thought maybe she caught something there. But we didn't know what was wrong with her." Ma Lila looked nonchalant. "I know I've told you this."

Kari shook her head. None of it sounded familiar at all.

"It was hepatitis. While she was in Gulf Shores, she went to one of those Mexican restaurants. Maybe the place wasn't too clean. Anyway—" Ma Lila picked up her glass. "It takes a long time to recover from hepatitis. And your mother was so depressed. You know how she hates being ill. And to have to see her friends having such a good time while she was convalescent in bed, well, I thought a change of scenery would be good for her. So I sent her to visit my sister in Knoxville. And she worked out an arrangement with her teachers to have her lessons sent to her, so she wouldn't fall behind. And your mother's so smart, she didn't fall behind a bit. By January, she had made a full recovery, and she came back to finish out the year with her friends.

"That's why she wasn't in the yearbook?"

Ma Lila nodded. "It must have been too late by the time she got back."

"Then why wasn't her name on the 'Not Pictured' list?"

Ma Lila shrugged. "I don't know. Must have been those editors. They were probably just careless."

"It's funny," Kari said. "It seems like I would've heard about that before."

"I'm sure you have, child," Ma Lila said. "Maybe you just forgot about it."

"I don't know—"

"In any event," Ma Lila said, "it was a long time ago. Now let's go see if we can find those gloves."

{ chapter*fifteen* }

SATURDAY AFTERNOON, SHAWNA FOUND her father on the back porch, grading papers. He sat in the rocking chair with an ankle crossed over his knee, tracing his pen down the page as he read carefully. Every now and then, he leaned over to write something in the margins. Shawna wasn't sure if she should disturb him; he looked completely engrossed in his essays. Is it enough, she wondered, to teach junior high kids American history, to talk about the Constitution, the Civil War, the Industrial Revolution year after year? Watching him reading his students' papers, Shawna tried to imagine Dad as Mom saw him. Did he seem unambitious to Mom, who made senior partner last year, won an award from the Colorado Bar Association? "That's right, go running home to your mother," she'd overheard Mom saying when her parents decided to separate.

"When are you going to grow up?" Shawna winced as she remembered. Was Dad just running home to Mommy? She wondered if he still loved her mother or missed her.

"Dad?" Her voice was almost a whisper.

He looked up. "Shawna. I didn't hear you come out."

"Busy?"

Dad wrote something in a margin, then set down his pile of essays. "The usual. You look like you have something on your mind."

Shawna thought for a moment, wondering how she should approach the subject. "Something—kind of weird."

"Sounds intriguing."

"Maybe. Remember that girl who broke the window?" Shawna shielded her eyes and looked out over the back yard. The sun cast a warm glow over the porch.

Dad grinned. "You're telling me you and Kari Lang have become friends?"

Shawna shrugged. She wouldn't exactly call them friends. "She told me something yesterday. She said she was looking through some old yearbooks but she didn't see you or her mother in the senior class. And I went to the public library this morning to check it out, and it's true. Neither one of you is in it."

"And you're wondering if we were both playing hooky on picture day?"

"When someone misses picture day, they usually get put in a list. But it was like you both disappeared from Dessina High School altogether."

Dad stopped rocking and sat still. "You're right."

"I'm right?"

"I never told you this before, but I never graduated from Dessina High."

Shawna felt her mouth fall open and she snapped it shut. "You didn't?"

"I graduated from Jefferson High up in Chicago. That's where I spent my senior year."

Shawna was speechless.

Dad had a wry look on his face. "You're wondering why you didn't know that?"

"Why didn't I know that?" Shawna stammered.

Dad sat back in his chair and rocked slowly. "It may have seemed like an important moment in the past, but in retrospect, it really wasn't. In fact, it was a pretty uneventful year." He leaned over and looked Shawna in the eye. "I liked Chicago. In fact, I liked it so much that I decided to go to college at Northwestern. And that's where I met your mother."

"You left because of Kari's mom?"

Dad sat still, without speaking. He looked deep in thought. Shawna watched him closely, but his expression told her nothing.

"There were misunderstandings, yes," he said finally. "And there's about a forty-eight-hour period of my life that I would never care to repeat. But listen to me when I say this." He leaned closer to Shawna. "It was my decision to finish out the year in Chicago."

"But why—" Shawna began, but Dad cut her off.

"You don't need to know everything there is to know about a person to be close," he said. "I'm sure there are episodes in your life that you haven't told me about."

Shawna lowered her eyes. "And you're saying that you won't tell me about this one?"

"You're one perceptive girl," Dad said with a smile.

"But if it was no big deal, then why—"

"Shawna—" he cut in, and Shawna detected an edge in his

voice. He had said all he would say. Shawna wanted to protest, but he shook his head.

"People get into trouble when they try to judge situations they know nothing about."

"So you're telling me to back off," Shawna muttered.

"That's right," Dad said. To prove his point, he picked up his students' essays. For a moment, Shawna watched her father's eyes as he scanned the page. It was like the conversation had never happened. But Kari had landed on something important; Shawna knew that. She wondered if her father knew her well enough to know that she wasn't about to back off from this. I'm a journalist, for goodness sake, she thought.

It was time to get in touch with Kari, see what Kari had learned. She went upstairs to her room, taking the phone book with her. There were three Langs in the phone book. The second listing was for a Steve and Allison, so Shawna dialed that number.

The phone rang only once before someone answered with an unmistakably Southern accent. "Hello?" The voice sounded like an older woman.

"May I please speak to Kari?"

"Kari's out of town," the voice said. "She went down to Jonesboro with her girlfriends. They're picking up their dresses."

"Dresses?" Shawna had no idea what the voice was talking about.

"For the ball," the voice said, as if Shawna should have known. "You don't sound like you're from Dessina. Are you a classmate of Kari's?"

"Yes, I am," Shawna said. "Can you tell her to call Shawna when she gets in?"

The voice repeated the number. "I'll give her the message."

"Thanks," Shawna said and hung up. The voice on the phone had sounded too old to be Kari's mother. It was funny, how surprised the voice was that Shawna didn't know the rituals associated with the ball. It then occurred to her that whoever it was probably assumed from her voice that she was white.

The phone rang and Shawna picked it up.

It was Sephora. "I'm over at Tashi's. You're coming to the revival, right?"

"Um." Shawna didn't know what to say.

"Because afterward, Tashi's having a huge party. I'm helping her get it set up right now. She's even got a DJ coming, and Eddie's here; he brought a whole bunch of Kappas from Morehouse with him. It's gonna be live—"

"I don't think so," Shawna said. How could she sit through a long church service with so much on her mind? And she wasn't sure if she was in the mood for a party.

"Shawna . . ." Sephora sounded disappointed.

"Sorry," Shawna said. "I'm not—feeling well."

Sephora let out a long, whistling sigh. "You'll miss out. See you Monday."

"Okay," Shawna said and hung up. Sephora was right; it would be a missed opportunity. Maybe she could have met some nice college boy tonight. But there was too much to think about. Too much she didn't know about her father.

When Shawna went downstairs again, Dad was gone. "He's at the basketball court," Grandma Rory said. She was carrying a large pot of string beans out to the back porch.

Shawna followed her. "Need some help?"

"Sure." Grandma Rory pushed the pot of beans between them. Shawna reached into the pot and picked out a few of the beans, rolling them between her hands. Grandma Rory's hands flew as she snapped the ends off the beans and transferred them to a large bowl.

"I was just talking to Dad," Shawna said. "He was telling me how he finished school in Chicago." She snapped the ends off of one of the beans and put it in her mouth. It had the grassy taste that Shawna associated with green vegetables, but it was sharp and crunchy.

Grandma Rory picked up another handful of beans and made quick work of snapping them and flicking them into the bowl. "It was July the sixth," she said. "Your Grandpa Joe called Chattanooga and ordered the ticket. I was packing a box for him to take on the bus. He took the ten-twelve bus to Chicago that night, on account of that girl."

"What happened?" Shawna asked.

Grandma Rory wiped her brow before picking up another handful of beans. "I don't know what was true and what was fiction. I don't think any of us do but your father and that girl. All I know was that he was gone for Fourth of July weekend. He said he was spending the weekend at his friend Samuel's house. Only time the boy ever lied to me. Next thing I know, on July the fourth I get a phone call from Amicalola Falls. It seems that girl's brother caught them up there together. When your father got home, I called my sister Ernestine up in Chicago. The night your father took the bus up to Chicago, I didn't stop praying until he called me from my sister's house." She fell quiet and the only sound was the snap of the beans and the sound they made as they landed in the pot.

"Dad didn't want to talk about it," Shawna said.

"I don't reckon there's much to say," Grandma Rory said. But then she frowned, looking angrier than Shawna had ever seen her look. "I'm gonna say this one time and then I'll keep my peace. I don't have one bit of respect for these little white girls who play with our boys like that."

"What would've happened if Dad didn't go to Chicago?"

Grandma stood up. "I just thank the Lord I never had to find out."

The clouds around the sun were deepening to pink and purple and the sun seemed to be perched right on top of the trees. Shawna faced the setting sun, shivering even though there was no breeze. She sat on the porch for a long time after her grandmother left. Dad would have been my age, she thought, sixteen. She imagined him sitting on the bus, probably crouched down low, out of sight. What was he thinking then? And Kari's mother, what had happened to her? Had she gone on her merry way, not even caring what happened to Dad?

Shawna went inside to call Kari again, but this time the voice told her that Kari hadn't come home, that she was spending the night at Clare's house. At Clare's, the voice said, as if Shawna was supposed to know exactly who that was. She hung up the phone and flung herself on the bed. So Kari had gone to buy her hoopskirt dress for the Old South Ball. Shawna pictured Kari with her friends as they swished and swayed in their dresses, and she remembered what Tashi had said about the little black kids acting as servants.

The editorial—Shawna brought a hand to her head and sat up. She still had the crumpled piece of paper Marlon had given her, even though she had already typed it up and formatted it for the newspaper. The paper was sitting next to her computer. Shawna picked it up. Smoothing it across her lap, she read it again.

THE OLD SOUTH BALL IN
BLACK AND WHITE
by Natalie Curran and Marlon Coleman

By now, it seems like everyone at school is on one side or the other as to whether the Old South Ball should remain a Dessina High School tradition. We've listened to arguments on both sides of the issue, but we feel like we have a different perspective to bring to the subject. The two of us met several weeks ago, outside of school. Maybe in school, we would have passed each other every day, without notice. But we grew to be good friends, and then decided we liked each other more than that. It's tough to have a relationship like we have, because so many people think that black people and white people shouldn't date each other. It's hard to see each other at school and act like we're just acquaintances even though we're more than that. But even though we know we might get dirty looks, and people might say things, we decided we wouldn't hide our feelings for each other anymore. And as we thought about this Old South Ball, we realized that maybe the issue isn't as black and white as it seems. Why can't there be compromise? Why can't the ball become a school event? So we consider this an open letter to the Parents' Auxiliary. Would we be turned away from the ball if we showed up together? And if so, then what kind of tradition does this ball really stand for?

Shawna reached for the phone and quickly dialed Marlon's number, but he wasn't home. Track meet in Augusta, his mother said. She hung up the phone, frustrated. She wanted to ask him if he was sure about this, if he still wanted her to sneak this editorial into the newspaper on Monday. Was this some kind of game to Natalie, some sort of whim? Did she even consider what this editorial could do to Marlon?

Shawna looked at the phone again, hesitating. But then she picked up the phone and dialed the number to her old house in Denver.

Mom answered the phone abruptly. "Hello?" She sounded hurried, like she was just about to run out or she had just come in the front door.

"Mom, it's me."

"Shawna. How are you doing?"

"Okay, I guess. Are you busy?"

"I was just on my way to the office, but I'm in no hurry. What's on your mind?"

"I wanted to ask your advice on something."

"What is it?"

"A friend of mine here, he—" Shawna took a deep breath. How should she explain it? "He's dating someone, just like I used to date Jordan."

"What about it?"

"Well, he and his girlfriend, they wrote an article for the newspaper about their relationship, but I'm not sure if I should put it in."

"What difference does it make?"

"It makes a lot of difference!" Shawna felt her face warming. "Remember how bad things ended up with Jordan?"

"Things didn't have to end badly with Jordan, Shawna."

"Mom, Jordan didn't want to be seen in public with me!" Shawna was almost shouting. She squeezed her eyes shut, wishing she had never brought it up.

"I think you're exaggerating a bit. I told you last time we talked that I saw him. Why would he still be asking about you if he didn't like you?"

"Mom, I don't want to talk about Jordan; I want to talk about what's going on here!"

Mom was silent.

"What do you think I should do? The white kids here, they put on something called an Old South Ball. They wear hoopskirts and Confederate uniforms and stuff. I wrote an article about it for the newspaper this week because I think it's time to just end things like that."

"I suppose that didn't go over well." Mom's tone was acid.

"Not really. But now my friend and his girlfriend, they wrote an article asking what would happen if they showed up at the ball together."

"Now why on earth would they want to do that?"

"To see what this tradition's really all about. So, Mom, what should I do?"

Mom was quiet for a long time. Then Shawna heard her sigh. "I never understood why your father wants to live in such a backward place."

Shawna didn't know what to say.

"I'm just sorry you had to learn the hard way. I hope this means you're thinking about coming home next year."

What is home for me? Shawna wondered, but she didn't say it out loud.

"You're a smart girl, Shawna; do what you think is right. Anyway, I need to be getting back to the office. Do you have enough money?"

"Yeah, I have enough."

"All right then. We'll talk soon."

Shawna hung up the phone, more confused than ever. She glanced at the crumpled paper, then lay down on her bed. There was nothing to do but wait. Wait and see what happened.

{ chapter *sixteen* }

HOW COULD KARI NOT be excited about the Spring Ball after the trip to Jonesboro? Even MC, who wasn't the kind of girl who showed much emotion about anything, giggled and squealed like Clare as they tried on their dresses Saturday night, experimented with makeup. The next two weeks would be frenetically busy. On Monday, all Dessina juniors and seniors would be officially invited to the prom. On Friday, the Etoiles would have a special meeting, where they would make boutonnieres for their prom dates. Prom on Saturday night began a full week of activities leading up to the Spring Ball. Each day there would be a different event: barbecues, ice cream socials, teas. And then, the Saturday after prom, the ball itself.

Monday morning at school, Kari saw Shawna waiting by

the front door. She went straight to Kari and said, "We have to talk."

"I'll see you next period," Kari said to MC and Clare, who looked at her curiously before going inside. Kari followed Shawna out to a grassy area by the parking lot.

"You learn something?" Shawna asked her.

Kari nodded. "What about you?"

"My dad didn't graduate from Dessina. That's why he wasn't in the yearbook."

"He didn't?"

"He spent his senior year in Chicago."

"My goodness," Kari breathed. "Why?"

Shawna looked a little angry. She twisted her purse strap in her fists. Coach, Kari noticed. On Saturday, she had looked at the Coach bags in the glass cases at Macy's. "He wouldn't tell me about it, so I had to ask my grandma." She glared at Kari. "Something was going on between your mom and my dad."

"What?" Kari felt her face coloring. "You mean—"

"Your family has a cabin in the mountains, right?"

Kari wondered how Shawna knew that.

"Well, I guess your mom and my dad went up there over Fourth of July or something and they got caught."

"Got caught, what do you mean, got caught?"

"I don't know, someone saw them up there!" Shawna raised her voice. "And when my dad got back, my grandma sent him to Chicago."

"My goodness—" Kari brought a hand to her mouth. "Because of Mom?"

"That's what my grandma said."

Kari shook her head, not knowing what to think.

"I called you three times."

"Nobody gave me the message," Kari said. Ma Lila was always forgetting to give Kari phone messages. "Well, if it's important, they'll call back," she always said, to Kari's annoyance.

"My grandma said that Mom got sick," Kari said. "Hepatitis. She went to Knoxville, to my aunt's house, to get better because she was so depressed about being sick."

"And you bought that?"

Kari felt foolish. Coming out of her mouth, it sounded like a lie. But Ma Lila had been so matter-of-fact. Like they were discussing the weather. Kari could usually spot her grandmother's lies a mile away. Her hands fluttered and her eyes shifted around, avoiding people. But she had looked right at Kari when she told her about her mother. "So you think my grandma lied to me?"

"What do you think? Your mom was sent away; my dad was sent away. That much we know. When did your mom get sent away?"

"I don't know," Kari said. "Ma Lila didn't say. She just said that Mom got sick sometime in summer."

"That must've been the lie they told everybody to explain why your mother went away."

"I guess so. But Mom came back."

Shawna looked up. "Came back?"

"In January. Grandma said she came back in January and finished out the year."

The first bell rang and Shawna jumped to her feet. She looked nervous. "I should be in newspaper already. But we need to talk again. When can we talk?"

"How about tonight?" Kari got up and followed Shawna into the building. Shawna walked quickly, like she was in a hurry. The entranceway was quiet; most students were already congesting the hallways, moving toward their first-period classes.

"When tonight?" Shawna asked.

"I'm usually done with dinner by seven," Kari said. "I'll come to your house."

"I'll be out in front. Oh." She stopped suddenly. "Have you told anyone about this?"

Kari shook her head. "Have you?"

"No," Shawna said. "Let's keep it that way for now." Before Kari could say anything else, Shawna hurried away.

Kari stood where she was for a moment, then moved slowly down the entranceway. She heard the second bell ring, and by the time she crossed the cafeteria, the halls were empty. When she got to study hall, she immediately crossed her arms on her desk and laid her head down. She tried to conjure up the junior pictures of Mom and Joe Riley, but all she could see in her head was who they were now. They were dating. Keeping the whole thing one big secret. They had to. If word had gotten around, then her mother would have been ruined. That's what Rick and Troy called it. Kari remembered a conversation they had several months ago about a girl rumored to be dating a black boy. MC had said that maybe the girl was dating him because she was curious. Troy turned up his nose and said, "What's to be curious about? They've got two legs and two arms, too."

"But if two people are in love—" MC said.

"Then they've gotta deal with all the people in town who're gonna talk," Rick said.

"So you're saying people shouldn't do it because other people will make it bad, or you're saying it just shouldn't be done?" MC asked.

No one had an answer for that, but Kari suspected that Troy and Rick both thought it just shouldn't be done.

What would Rick think if he knew about Mom? What

would he say if he knew Kari's mom had been sent away because she'd spent the night alone with a black boy? Ma Lila played it cool, Kari realized, cool as a cucumber. She made up the story about hepatitis. And did her own father know? Daddy was two years younger than Mom; he would have been a lowly freshman when all of this was happening. Kari tried to think of anything specific Daddy had said about black people, or about race in general, but she couldn't think of anything. Her father was the type who would fall silent when conversations turned political.

But Mom. Kari rubbed her forehead. What would it be like to go away with Joe Riley, knowing what people would think of her when they found out? She must've really liked him. Maybe she even loved him. Wouldn't you have to love someone to go through with something like that?

{ chapter *seventeen* }

KARI DIDN'T GET IT. To her, it was probably all some stupid thing to laugh about with her Etoile Club friends. C'mon, that's not fair, Shawna told herself. But she couldn't help thinking it. She couldn't help picturing Kari and her friends swishing around in ball gowns while little black kids served them punch and cake. And her mother, coming back to Dessina while Dad was put on a bus to Chicago. And now Marlon and Natalie's stupid editorial—Shawna brought her hand to her head. What could Marlon possibly have been thinking? And what had she been thinking for agreeing to help them?

Sephora was sitting against the locker when Shawna approached. A book was opened in front of her and she sucked on a lollipop. "By the way, Marlon was just here, looking for you."

"Marlon?" Shawna repeated.

Sephora grinned. "He seemed kinda nervous, like he really wanted to talk to you about something. Maybe he's asking you to the prom."

"No, he wasn't going to ask me to the prom," Shawna said, irritated.

"How do you know?" Sephora said. "I mean, it's sort of the last minute, but—"

"Because he's going with someone else, okay?"

Sephora stood up, looking worried. "You know that for sure?"

Shawna nodded.

"Who is she?"

Shawna felt her eyes narrowing as she thought of Natalie. "You'll find out soon enough."

"Shawna—"

"Listen," Shawna said. "I've got to go find Marlon, okay? I'll see you later."

Sephora shrugged. "Whatever."

Shawna hurried over to Mrs. Richter's classroom, her heart pounding. Why am I so uptight? she wondered. It was Marlon and Natalie's problem, wasn't it? But it was so much more than that. It made Shawna dizzy to think about it.

Marlon was sitting on the floor outside of the room. "Shawna—"

"Hi, Marlon," she said.

He looked anxious.

"Where's Natalie?" Shawna thought she sounded a little snide, but she didn't care.

"She's got math first period," he said. "Are you going to—"

Shawna cut him off. "You know I will."

He stared at her. "Is everything all right?"

Shawna blinked. "How can you ask me that? No, everything's not all right!"

Marlon glanced around him and Shawna immediately shut her mouth.

"Look, something's been bugging you," he said. "Wanna talk about it?"

Shawna sat on the floor next to him. For a second she looked at his shoulder. Wouldn't it be wonderful to snuggle up there and—she made herself cut off the thought. "Aren't you scared?"

"Honestly?" Marlon said. "No."

Shawna shook her head quickly. "This isn't an afterschool movie or something, Marlon! You honestly don't know what's gonna happen tomorrow after the article comes out."

Marlon smiled. "We're not the first people to do what we're doing."

"No." Shawna stared at the carpet. She thought of Dad and Allison Lang. "No, you're not."

"And don't forget, I've lived here all my life. This isn't Klansville; it's not really like that. Some people might not get it—"

"You really like her, don't you?"

"Yeah." It was such a simple answer. When would it stop hurting to think of him with Natalie? Without meaning to, Shawna leaned against him. She was about to jerk herself upright when she felt Marlon put his arm around her shoulder. She felt his lips pressing against the side of her head, and the hallway went blurry.

"We'd better go in soon," he said.

She nodded without speaking. If she opened her mouth, she'd certainly cry.

They stood up and went into the classroom. Mrs. Richter was talking with Troy. The rest of the staff were scattered around the room. Shawna threw herself into the day's work, finalizing the layout before the paper went to the printer's at noon. She had already measured out the pro/con Old South Ball section against Natalie and Marlon's editorial. All that was left to do was actually insert the article after class.

When the bell rang, Shawna wandered around the room until everyone left. Mrs. Richter always went to the teacher's lounge between first and second periods. All Shawna needed was two minutes, and the deed was done.

She left the room quickly. She realized she had forgotten her science folder, so she hurried in the opposite direction to her locker. Up ahead, she saw Natalie turning the corner, walking toward her. Shawna stopped where she was, looking directly at Natalie. Natalie must have felt her glare because she turned toward Shawna and for a moment, they stared at each other.

Shawna felt her jaw clench. You better care about him as much as he cares about you, she thought. She was giving Natalie a dirty look; she knew it. But she couldn't help it. Natalie looked nervous. She lowered her eyes and walked past Shawna, saying nothing.

Shawna grabbed a notebook from her locker and hurried over to the science wing, taking her seat right as the bell rang. But as she went to her lab station, she realized she had grabbed her history folder by mistake. During the lab, she spilled the saline solution and the teacher made a big fuss, making everyone stand back while the mess was cleaned up.

During class, she could feel MC looking at her. She imagined MC was wondering what was going on between Shawna and Kari. What a silly story Kari's grandmother told her about her mom, Shawna thought. Hepatitis? But if not hepatitis, then what?

"Oh, my God," Shawna said under her breath. Only one thing made sense.

chapter *eighteen*

BEFORE LAST PERIOD, CLARE caught up with Kari at their locker. "Are you mad at me?"

"Mad at you? Why would I be mad at you?" Kari asked, annoyed.

"I don't know; you've been in this funk all day."

Kari sighed. "I just have a lot on my mind."

"Is it that girl?" Clare said. "Every time you go off with her, you always get upset."

"There's just something going on that I can't talk about."

"Something you can't tell me?"

"Maybe I'll tell you soon, but for now, I gotta deal with this myself."

Clare looked suspicious. "And that girl, she's got something to do with it."

Kari nodded slightly.

Clare grew angry. "Is it something about the ball? Has she got you upset about it?"

Kari shook her head quickly. "It's nothing like that. I'm going to be late; I have to go."

Kari was late. The bell rang when she was still a ways from her French class.

Kari usually liked French. Her teacher said she had a good accent. It was the only class Kari had where students sometimes asked her for help. Today, Kari didn't want to recite dialogues or conjugate verbs. She sat morose, staring at the clock, willing the hands to crawl faster toward the final bell.

When school was over for the day, Kari gathered her books and hurried out of the room.

Kessler was waiting there, pacing impatiently. Kari was surprised to see her. She never spoke to Kessler unless there was Etoile business to discuss.

"Kari." Kessler looked furious about something, and for a panicky second Kari wondered if she had done something wrong. "Emergency meeting at Jolie's. Four o'clock. Mandatory." She was gone before Kari could respond.

Mandatory meeting? She figured MC or Clare would know what was up, but on the way to their locker, she saw Rick and Troy coming toward her from the opposite direction. Troy carried a folded newspaper in his hands.

"I can't believe she did this!" Troy was exclaiming.

"What's going on?" Kari asked.

Instead of putting his arm around her, Rick simply glared at her. "Your new best friend, look at what she did."

Troy thrust the newspaper at Kari. She fumbled with it for a moment. The *Dessina Weekly Journal*, dated tomorrow. Troy had the paper open to the editorial page. Kari looked for Shawna's column, figuring all the trouble would be there, but instead, there was something else.

THE OLD SOUTH BALL IN BLACK AND WHITE
by Natalie Curran and Marlon Coleman

"My goodness—" Natalie and Marlon? So MC had been right after all.

"Can you believe it?" Troy looked so angry Kari thought he would slam his fist into a locker.

Rick was still glaring at Kari, standing apart from her, like he wanted nothing to do with her. "You know what I think?" he said. "I think that girl Shawna's behind this. This is her way of trying to end the ball."

"How?" Kari asked.

Rick brought a hand to his forehead and rolled his eyes, like he thought Kari was an idiot. "If the Parents' Auxiliary says no, then all the black parents get up in arms and call them racist and march and protest and get the NAACP or something. And if they say yes—" He stopped and turned to Kari. "You don't look all that surprised."

"What?"

Rick's eyes narrowed at her. "You've been mighty buddy-buddy with Shawna lately."

"I didn't know anything about this!"

Rick looked like he didn't believe her.

"I don't even know Marlon!"

"But you know Shawna," Troy put in. "Marlon couldn't have done this without her."

"This is great." Rick threw up his hands. "Now I can't even trust my own girlfriend?"

"But—" Kari couldn't find any words to say.

"So you're saying you don't want to go to the ball with me?" Rick's voice sounded cold.

"But we got our dresses on Saturday!" Kari protested, wanting to cry. "How could you think I—" Tears came to her eyes. "Shawna and me, it's got nothing to do with the ball. I don't know anything about this!"

She was crying. Rick and Troy stood there uncomfortably as Kari sniffled and wiped her eyes. Once she started crying, she couldn't stop. Why am I so upset? she wondered, but then she couldn't think anymore and leaned against the lockers. She covered her face with her hands and sobbed.

"I'm sorry." Kari felt Rick's arms around her and she buried her head in his shoulder. "Please don't cry."

Kari hiccuped and choked back her tears. Rick held up a handkerchief and Kari wiped her face and blew her nose.

"Can you give me a ride to Jolie's?" she asked, her voice shaky.

"Sure," Rick mumbled.

"So much for your new member," Troy said.

Kari didn't answer. She felt exhausted. She swiped a hand under her eyes and took a deep breath. Rick put an arm around her and they walked out to the parking lot.

"Something's got you real upset," he said when they got to his car. "And I wanna know about it."

Kari sighed and looked in the mirror. She looked awful: Her face was blotchy and her eyes red. She didn't want to go to some stupid meeting at Jolie's. She wanted to go home, be alone.

"Will you talk to me?" Rick asked.

"I can't."

Rick didn't say anything else on the ride to Jolie's and Kari was grateful for that. She knew he hated to see her cry.

"Bye," Kari said as she got out of the car, not kissing him. She just wanted to get the meeting over with so that she could talk to Shawna.

There was no Bettina to greet her at the door today, no cookies and tea set out. Everyone was already there as Kari entered. Clare and MC had saved her a seat, and she sat down without saying a word. She could feel MC and Clare looking at her. She knew they were wondering why she had been crying, but there was no time to say anything because the meeting had begun. As she expected, Natalie Curran was nowhere to be seen.

"We're all here," Jolie said, glaring at Kari.

Kari felt her face redden and she frowned at the floor.

Jolie stood at the front of the room, looking at each member in turn. "As you all know, Natalie Curran was supposed to be our newest member—"

Jolie paused and Kari wondered what she would say.

"She has placed herself with those who wish to end the ball," Jolie said.

"She also made a fool of you," Kari heard MC say under her breath. Kari giggled and clamped a hand over her mouth as Jolie glared at her, outraged. But Kari saw a smile at the corner of MC's mouth. Kari coughed to make it look like an accident. Only Clare looked grave.

"As I was saying," Jolie said, "I think that we as a club ought to distance ourselves from Natalie Curran. So I propose that we take back our offer of membership."

"Second," Kessler said.

"So we'll put it to a vote," Jolie said. "All in favor?"

A persistent rapping at the door caught Jolie's attention. She looked around for a moment, like she was expecting Bettina to answer the door.

"I'll get it." Kessler jumped up and went to the door.

Kari, MC, and Clare all looked at each other and the girls began to murmur among themselves.

"—Kari Lang—"

Kari stood up at the sound of her name.

A few moments later, Shawna Riley walked into the room. Several of the girls gasped in surprise, including Clare. Kessler followed, looking annoyed.

"Shawna?" Kari said.

Jolie looked Shawna up and down. "We're in the middle of a private meeting."

Shawna ignored her, looking at Kari. "It's an emergency. We have to talk."

"An emergency," Kessler repeated. "A right-this-minute emergency?"

Shawna looked impatient. "Are you coming?"

Kari felt the eyes of the entire Etoile Club on her. Clare stared at her, openmouthed. Jolie and Kessler looked at her with arms crossed. Kari was short of breath.

"Kari?" Clare looked apprehensive.

Before she knew it, Kari was crossing the room and she and Shawna were out the front door.

Once outside, Kari breathed deeply. "What are you doing here?"

"Come on." Shawna's car was parked in front. In the car, Shawna turned to Kari. "I saw Troy and he told me there was an emergency meeting."

"Yeah—"

Shawna smiled a little. "Did they kick Natalie out yet?"

"Of course," Kari said. "That was something, what you put in the paper."

Shawna shrugged. "I didn't write it. Marlon and Natalie did. It was their idea."

"Well, my boyfriend thought I had something to do with it."

"Why would he think that?"

"He knows we've been talking!" Kari retorted. "So what's all this about?"

"I've been thinking about our parents all day. I can't get it out of my head."

"Me neither," Kari said.

"What you said about your mom, that she was sent to Tennessee—" Shawna began. "We know she didn't have hepatitis, but what if it was something else?"

"What do you mean?"

"What if your mom was pregnant?"

"Pregnant!" Kari shouted. It was almost an insult.

"Think about it!" Shawna spoke quickly, excitedly. "Why else would she have to be sent away? My dad was already gone; nobody had to know they went to the cabin together."

"But—"

"And she came back in January," Shawna said. "So let's say she got pregnant in the spring, during the school year—"

Kari's face was hot. "She'd start showing by the summer."

"Haven't you heard stories about how girls used to get sent away when they got pregnant?"

"You really think—"

"Why else would your mom be sent away? I can't think of any other reason."

"Jesus Christ." Kari had been taught not to take the Lord's name in vain, but it flew out of her mouth.

"She couldn't have had an abortion. Not legally, anyway."

Kari brought a hand to her mouth. "So you think she had a baby?"

Shawna was breathing deeply. "Which means we have a brother or sister out there somewhere."

Kari sucked in her breath so hard she could feel the air whooshing in her lungs. But when she let her breath out, she felt herself smiling. Her face was warm and her vision blurred and suddenly she was crying and laughing at the same time.

"I've never had a brother or sister." Shawna was crying and laughing, too.

"Me neither." Kari's hands were shaking in her lap. Without thinking, she reached out, then pulled back, hesitating. But Shawna got the hint and reached out as well. And when their hands clasped together, they were crying, which made them both start laughing hysterically until they fell back in their seats, breathless.

"So what are we gonna do now?" Kari asked.

"I don't know," Shawna said, catching her breath.

"Do we ask our parents?"

Shawna thought for a minute, then shook her head. "My dad didn't want to talk about it."

"My mom never talks to me about anything—"

Shawna turned quickly to Kari. "Let's go."

"Go," Kari said. "Go where?"

"Let's find out for ourselves."

Kari blinked. "You mean, go to Tennessee, go to Knoxville?"

Shawna just smiled.

Kari nodded. It made sense. It made more sense than anything Kari knew.

"All right," she said. "Let's go."

{ part *two* }

{ chapter *nineteen* }

"WE'LL STOP AT YOUR house first," Shawna said.

Instead of looking excited, Kari was staring at the dashboard, frowning.

"You still want to go, right?" Shawna asked, hearing an edge in her own voice.

Kari nodded vigorously. "Turn left up here. I was just thinking—" Her voice trailed.

"What?"

"What are we gonna tell our folks?"

Shawna listened to the hum of the car engine. "We'll call them when we get to Knoxville. That way they'll know where we are."

"I don't have much money."

"I have a credit card."

Kari looked up. "Really?"

"It's for emergencies. This counts as an emergency, don't you think?"

"I guess so." Kari motioned for Shawna to turn again and Shawna entered a neighborhood of close-spaced, smallish houses. The houses looked like they'd seen many generations of the same families growing up and growing old.

"Up ahead," Kari said. Shawna drove into a cul-de-sac. At the end of the cul-de-sac was a little yellow frame house with a dogwood tree in the front yard. The front lawn was bright green and well tended, with rows of pretty red flowers growing along the front walk.

"Um." Kari's face pinked.

"I'll wait out here for you."

"I won't be long." Kari closed the car door behind her and went into the house.

Leaving the engine running, Shawna surveyed the street. It seemed like a nice enough neighborhood. A few standard-looking cars were parked in driveways; some dusty-looking trucks lined the street. Shawna looked at Kari's house. Cute, she thought. No, quaint. She imagined the inside was bright and grandmotherish. Didn't Kari say her grandmother lived with them? I'll bet they have doilies on their tables, she thought. Kari's grandmother, at least on the phone, sounded like the type of person who would put doilies under lamps. Did Kari ever say what her parents did? Shawna couldn't remember if she had.

Kari came out of the house carrying a duffel bag. She had changed clothes; she wore jeans and a University of Georgia sweat shirt. Throwing the duffel bag in the backseat, Kari jumped into the car. "I have my Aunt Cora's address in Knoxville." Kari sounded out of breath. "And her phone number. I figure we can call her when we get to Knoxville and get directions."

"Do you know how to get to Knoxville?"

Kari shook her head.

"We'll have to buy a map." Shawna put the car in reverse. "How do I get out of here?"

Kari gave her directions to Old Dessina Road. Shawna was surprised at how close they lived to one another. In less than five minutes she was climbing the hill to her house.

"I'll wait out here for you," Kari said when Shawna parked in the driveway. Her father's car wasn't there. He wouldn't be home from school for another hour or so. But Grandma Rory's sedan was parked in front of her.

"What?" Shawna said, distracted.

"I'll wait out here for you."

"Okay." Shawna left the car running as she went up the stairs to the porch. She stood in the doorway for a moment, listening. She could hear clanging noises coming from the back of the house and figured Grandma Rory was in the kitchen. She ran up the stairs to her room.

"What do I need?" she said aloud. She emptied her book bag and began shoving clothes into it. "Underwear, jeans, shirts—" How much was enough? How long would they be gone? Don't forget the Visa card, she told herself. She could always buy anything they needed. Going into the bathroom, she threw her toothbrush, a towel, and a washcloth into the bag. The zipper strained as she pulled it tight. She hoped it wouldn't break.

"Shawna, you here?" she heard Grandma Rory calling up the back stairs.

"Yeah," Shawna said. "I'm on my way out. I'll be home later." It's not a complete lie, she told herself. She opened her purse and took out her wallet. Credit card was there. They were set. Shawna hurried down the stairs and out to the car.

Kari slouched in the front seat, her feet resting against the dashboard. She had gathered her hair into a ponytail. She sat up as Shawna got into the driver's seat. Her eyes glittered and she looked excited. "Ready to go?"

"Ready." Shawna backed onto the street. She wasn't exactly sure where they were going or the best way to get there. She figured she would stop at the gas station at the top of the hill, buy a map, and navigate their way from there. There was a lot to talk about, a lot to say. A brother or a sister they had between them. The idea was still almost too incredible to believe. Looking at Kari, Shawna didn't know what to think. They hardly knew each other at all, and now, they might be family.

Shawna felt almost light-headed as the car crested the hill. They were going on an adventure. She could hardly think of anything else.

{ chapter *twenty* }

AN HOUR INTO THE drive, neither Shawna nor Kari had said much. Every few minutes or so, Kari would steal a glance at Shawna and see her eyes fixed on the road. The radio played, low and soft. Shawna didn't look happy, or sad, or nervous, or scared, or excited. She just drove. The longer she drove, the more expression melted from her face until her face just looked tight—closed off—like she was thinking about something and didn't want Kari to know about it.

Kari sat up in her seat, feeling the wind slapping her face, her ponytail streaming behind her. She was glad she had brought something for her hair. But it was hard to remember much about anything else. She couldn't remember what she was thinking about when Shawna walked into that Etoile Club meeting, or when she was in her house gathering her things for the trip. Did I bring my toothbrush or underwear? she wondered. But Shawna had a credit card. Shawna would take care of things.

The sun had deepened to a burnt orange, and it seemed to sit right in front of them. Chattanooga was coming up, and then they would veer off onto Interstate 75, which would take them directly to Knoxville. "An easy drive," Shawna said when they stopped to gas up. She had bought a map and it took only moments to chart their course.

Kari twisted her hands in her lap, clasping them together, pulling them apart, digging her fingernails into her skin until little red crescent moons appeared on her palms. Her lips were dry, and she wondered if she had some Chap Stick somewhere. The WELCOME TO TENNESSEE sign loomed ahead. She felt her heartbeat deep in her chest, like her heart had ballooned to fill her entire ribcage. Relax, Kari, she tried to tell herself. She wondered when her parents would realize she was gone. Mom was at the hospital; she probably wouldn't notice anything until tomorrow. And Daddy would come home from work and figure she was with Rick or with MC and Clare. Ma Lila—Kari frowned, thinking of Ma Lila. She might worry. She might even call MC or Clare, who would tell her about Kari leaving the Etoile Club meeting with Shawna Riley. And Ma Lila would go into a panic and probably call Mom at work, getting everyone all upset before she had a chance to call from Aunt Cora's house in Knoxville.

But then all the worry disappeared, just like the trees whizzing by. Getting in trouble, it didn't matter. She and Shawna had more important things to think about. Kari looked at herself in the side mirror. Her face was wind-whipped pink but other than that, she looked calm, like she knew exactly what she was doing and where she was going.

Kari slid down a little in her seat to avoid the wind. Looking up at the sky, she watched white puffs of clouds overhead drifting in the same direction as the car. She could count on two hands the number of car trips she'd ever made. Why didn't Mom and Daddy ever want to go anywhere? she wondered. They did have the cabin at Amicalola Falls, about an hour from Dessina, up in the mountains. Daddy and his friends would go deer hunting there in the fall and trout fishing in the spring. Mom went sometimes, although now it didn't make any sense why she did. It must have been a horrible scene, getting caught up there with Joe Riley. Kari didn't understand it at all. But that's why we're here, Kari thought. Excitement rose from her stomach up to her chest.

Will Aunt Cora recognize me? she thought suddenly. Of course she would, even though Kari was ten years old the last time she saw Aunt Cora. She had come to Knoxville unwillingly then; Aunt Cora was sick in the hospital with cancer and Ma Lila thought she would die. But she didn't die, and Kari spent two weeks sitting in a hospital ward when she could have gone to Hilton Head Island with Clare and her family. Aunt Cora would surely know Kari now; Kari was certain Ma Lila sent her pictures, told Aunt Cora about Rick and Etoiles and the Spring Ball.

There was so much she wasn't thinking about, so many things crammed into the corners of her mind trying to come center stage and get her attention. Her mother had a baby with Shawna's father. The thought was enough to make her heart feel swollen, pounding so hard it actually hurt. Her mom had sex and got pregnant. She had a baby and then gave it away, all before she turned seventeen. What would I do if I got pregnant? she thought. Rick would want to marry her. And he'd go back to school senior year and Kari would transfer to

Tolbert County High, where girls from Dessina went if they got pregnant. At Tolbert County, they went to school half the day like everyone else, and the other half of the day they learned how to take care of their babies. One of Clare's cousins went there.

Kari placed her hands on her stomach and pressed until she could feel her bottom ribs. I would be Mrs. Rick Durham and maybe the Etoiles would throw me a baby shower, she thought. Maybe some of the Etoiles would even be jealous: Kari with a wedding ring, getting so much attention. But then the thought darkened and Kari gasped. It wasn't like Mom could marry Joe Riley without her family turning its back on her. There wasn't a place for pregnant girls to go to school back then. And then there would be all the talk. Ma Lila—the Belle of the Ball when she was at Dessina High—disgraced by her daughter.

She shut her eyes and pictured Mom behind her eyelids. She could see the ash-blonde hair and the doctor's coat. More than anything, she could see Mom's placid, preoccupied expression. Kari imagined herself sitting next to Mom, the way she always stiffened when Mom came into a room, the way she always had to search for something to say. And she remembered the relief she always felt when Mom would leave.

I've spent my whole life avoiding my mother, Kari thought as her eyes opened. Mom was a doctor, someone who saved lives. She was a woman of the world, not a woman of Dessina, like Ma Lila. Isn't that what you want, Kari? a voice asked inside her. Didn't she want to be someone important, who did things that mattered to other people? Someone who had something at stake in her life besides what dress to wear to a ball?

She looked over at Shawna, whose hand rested on the stick

shift. Shawna mattered. She went out on a limb with her newspaper column. People knew who she was. People asked her what she thought about things. Next year, when they did all the Senior Class Most Likely To— voting, Shawna would be Most Likely to Succeed, Most Likely to Be Famous. And me, Kari wondered, what would I be? Most likely to be a housewife in Dessina, going to Etoile Club alumni luncheons—

No—she almost said it aloud. Mom had gotten pregnant and had a baby back when girls didn't do things like that or if they did, they got married and dropped out of school. And if they got pregnant by a black boy, nobody'd speak to them again. But Mom wasn't ruined. She went through God knows what and she still finished school, went to college, became a doctor. And Joe Riley, he became a teacher. And now, Shawna and Kari would find their brother or sister. I have something at stake, too, she thought. Something that really matters.

The first stars appeared through the clouds and the Smoky Mountains rose up all around them, descending into lakes still as ice. Kari felt the skin on her arms prickling. They were going to do something important. The Etoile Club and the Spring Ball were as insubstantial as smoke in her mind. All she knew was the present moment, listening to the tires on the road, feeling the cool rush of wind tickling the hair against her ears.

{ chapter *twenty-one* }

IT WAS EIGHT O'CLOCK when they reached Knoxville city limits. Shawna looked over at Kari, whose eyes were wide and apprehensive-looking. Shawna realized she was shivering. They had driven the whole way without stopping and with the top down.

"We need gas," she said.

Kari's head bobbed slightly. "And I need to call Aunt Cora."

Shawna drove into a 7-Eleven and filled up the car while Kari went to a pay phone. It was a warm night, slightly humid. Her neck felt sweaty and she waved away some insects buzzing around her face. The gas station smelled smoggy, like car exhaust sitting in one place for a long time. She used her credit card to pay for the gas at the pump, then licked her dry lips. She considered going inside to buy a soda, but then her knees locked up. She leaned against the car, breathing deeply.

Kari had her back to Shawna and she held one hand against her ear to shut out the outside noise. They hadn't talked much over the trip. Shawna watched the road mostly, her mind surprisingly clear. She had so many things to think about that all of her thoughts seemed to collapse into numbness. And in that numbness she had the same sense of discomfort she had felt nine months ago, following Dad's car as they drove from Colorado to Dessina. It began once they hit Kentucky, heightening as they crossed into Tennessee and then into Georgia. She was aware of her own skin color and became acutely aware of the skin color of everyone else. She wasn't sure why, exactly. Maybe it was noticing for the first time those funny little statues of black men in riding clothes along the sides of rest stops. Lawn jockeys, Dad told her they were called. She found their smiling faces and protruding eyes disturbing. It wasn't like she was expecting something to happen—to be refused service in a restaurant or a hotel. Maybe it was just the thought that there had been a time in Dad's life when he wasn't allowed into the hotels where they stayed or into the restaurants where they ate.

She was surprised she had that same edgy feeling now, nine months later. It must be this trip itself, she thought. The reason they were here in the first place.

Kari still stood at the pay phone. What if her aunt wasn't home? But then Shawna remembered the credit card. They could stay in any hotel they wanted to. She bounced on her heels, wishing Kari would hurry up. She wondered if Dad and Grandma Rory knew she was gone. Maybe they thought she was with Marlon somewhere or with Sephora. She wanted to hurry up and get where they were going so she could call, let them know she was all right.

Marlon. Shawna sucked in her breath. The editorial would come out tomorrow and she wouldn't be there. Marlon and his girlfriend would have to face the music without her. Endure the stares and the comments and maybe even— Shawna cut off the thought. Her throat felt like it was stuffed with cotton. She needed a drink.

She went into the store and bought the largest Coke she could. On the way out, she stopped by the phone booth, where Kari still stood with the phone against her ear. "What'd you say? Make a right turn where?" she was saying. Shawna figured everything was all right and went to sit in the front seat. She sipped the Coke but fought to swallow it down. Her skin felt damp and clammy. When did my life get so confusing? she thought. Was there a single moment when everything seemed to turn inside out? Or maybe that moment was happening right this instant as she felt the leather under her sweaty legs, her lips around the plastic straw, her hands grasping the paper cup, her fingertips moist with condensation. Marlon and Natalie, Dad and Allison Lang, and now Kari and Shawna, all spiraling together toward some destiny Shawna couldn't fathom. She couldn't even imagine that she had a brother or sister, living and breathing somewhere.

This might only be the beginning, her logical side told her. That sibling would be in his or her twenties now, maybe with a family, maybe living in another state. But even if it was the beginning, even if it took years to find him or her, she and Kari had landed onto an important truth that opened up a whole universe of possibilities.

She remembered Dad sitting out on the back porch grading papers. "You don't have to know everything about people to love them," she could hear him saying. And she was about to learn about a whole other life of his that she had never considered possible. Does Mom know about any of this? she wondered suddenly.

Kari came around to her side of the car. Shawna lowered the window. "What?"

"Maybe I should drive," Kari said. "It's sort of complicated."

"Can you drive a stick shift?"

Kari nodded, looking impatient. Shawna moved to the passenger seat, a little surprised. She had assumed she would be in charge of everything, with Kari following along.

Kari brushed her bangs off her face and let off a short sigh. Shawna watched her adjust the seat and mirrors. "Aunt Cora's in a tiff. She kept fussing at me, asking me what I'm doing here. It took forever to get the directions out of her." But when she looked at Shawna, she was smiling. "I didn't tell her about you."

Shawna felt the discomfort coming back as she chewed on the straw. She hadn't thought about that. What if Kari's aunt was some sort of racist and wouldn't let Shawna into the house? After all, isn't that why Kari's mom had to go away, to hide the fact she was pregnant by a black boy? If she is racist, Shawna thought, sitting up taller, then Kari and I will stay at a hotel. And it will be an expensive one.

Kari shrugged. "I thought it might be better to surprise her. I thought we might learn more that way. About Mom, I mean."

Shawna nodded. Kari had a point there. She watched the grid of city lights blinking over the city of Knoxville as Kari made a series of turns onto different roads. Shawna couldn't tell much about what Knoxville looked like. In the night, it looked like it could be any city.

Kari turned onto a street into an older-looking neighborhood, similar to the neighborhood where Kari lived in Dessina. Single-story frame houses sat on small lawns. Many houses had large, old-model sedans parked out front. "The number's seven-twelve," Kari said. "It should be up on the left." The numbers on the houses were hard to see, but soon Kari was pulling in front of a white house with thick bushes planted along the porch. For a moment they both sat there, staring at the dashboard. Shawna's mouth still felt dry, even though she had nearly finished her drink. Then Kari looked over at Shawna, a hint of a smile on her face. "Ready?"

Shawna took a deep breath and nodded. "Ready."

chapter *twenty-two*

AUNT CORA DIDN'T SEE her at first. Shawna stood on the front porch, off to one side, while Kari rang the doorbell. They didn't plan it that way; Shawna just stepped aside while Kari waited for someone to open the door. As they waited, Shawna's eyes traced the porch rail, the splinters of wood showing brown under flaked-away white paint. The house, in contrast, gleamed white like it had been recently painted.

A smile appeared on Kari's face as the door creaked open, a kind of pasted-on smile reserved for seldom-seen relatives. "Hi, Aunt Cora." She leaned over to give a smallish older woman a kiss on the cheek.

And then Aunt Cora was looking Shawna in the face.

She wasn't as old as Shawna expected. She was about

Shawna's height, and her back curved slightly. Her hair was deep brown and longer than most older women wore their hair. Shawna saw a faint family resemblance between Kari and her Aunt Cora.

"This is Shawna Riley," Kari said. "She made the trip with me."

Aunt Cora didn't smile. She didn't have any discernible expression on her face, nothing that showed how she felt about having a black girl on her doorstep. Shawna felt herself smiling. "It's nice to meet you, Mrs.—" She stopped, realizing she had no idea how to address her.

"Just call me Aunt Cora," she said. She didn't sound all that friendly when she said it. She stepped aside to let the girls in.

For a moment, they stood in the entranceway. From where she stood, Shawna could look into a small front room on her left, fussily decorated with knickknacks and family photographs, a dining room on her right, and down a short hall in front of her to a kitchen.

"I have to say, I wasn't expecting company tonight," Aunt Cora said, looking down at her bathrobe and slippers. She kept glancing at Shawna in a way that made her stand up straighter and paste a smile on her face like Kari. Aunt Cora wasn't studying her, but looked her way every now and then, like she was taking snapshots to study later.

"I reckon you're wondering what we're doing here," Kari said.

"You can tell me that over supper. But before you do anything, I want you to call your Ma Lila and tell her where you are." Again, Aunt Cora glanced at Shawna. "I imagine her people want to know where she is, too. Use the phone in that room there."

Aunt Cora went back to the kitchen and Shawna exhaled deeply, like she had been holding her breath. "What now?" For some reason, she thought it best to whisper.

"I don't know," Kari whispered back. "I guess we call our folks like Aunt Cora said." She looked as nervous as Shawna felt. It made Shawna feel better to see that.

In the living room, Shawna sat on a slippery velvet couch, watching Kari dial on the rotary telephone. Shawna looked around the room at pictures of family members hanging on the walls and propped in heavy-looking silver frames on little tables. Some of the pictures were of Kari at various ages. A dusty piano with yellow keys stood in the corner. It looked neglected, like no one had played it in a long time.

"Ma Lila—yes, we're at Aunt Cora's—we're fine—" Kari waited while, Shawna presumed, she was barraged with questions. "Can you put Mom on the phone?" She made a face at Shawna. Shawna stifled a laugh.

"Mom." The smile faded from Kari's face. "Just listen to me. I'm at Aunt Cora's because I—" She faltered, lowered her eyes.

"Just listen to me!" She sounded edgy. "I'm here with Shawna Riley. We know about you and her dad, and that's why we're here."

Kari had been twirling the telephone cord around her fingers, but now she gripped it tight. "What do you mean, you don't know what I'm talking about? Why can't you just say it?"

Shawna felt her own pulse rise as she watched Kari, Kari's face as taut as the telephone cord she clenched in her fist.

"The baby!" Kari exclaimed. "We know about the baby!"

Kari was silent for a moment. Her face loosened and she let the telephone cord fall from her fingers. "Fine. But we're here now and we're gonna find out what happened." She glanced at Shawna like she was looking for support. Shawna nodded quickly, which made Kari smile.

"As long as it takes," she said, then hung up. Kari slumped into the couch. "Whew!"

Shawna scooted closer. "What did she say?"

"Not much." Kari ran a hand over her forehead. Kari seemed different. She looked Shawna in the eye with her jaw rigid—no hunched shoulders, no looking at the floor.

"Why don't you call your dad," Kari said.

They switched places on the couch, and Shawna dialed her number as quickly as the rotary phone would allow.

Dad answered the phone.

"Dad?" Before he could say anything else, Shawna said, "I'm in Tennessee. Knoxville. With Kari Lang."

Dad was silent.

"We're in Knoxville because—" Shawna heard her voice wavering. Kari leaned toward her, nodding. It was more encouraging than she imagined. She sat up straighter. "Because we know about you and Kari's mom."

She heard Dad taking a deep breath. "Shawna—"

"We understand everything. Why she was sent here, why you were sent to Chicago."

"And what do you understand?" He didn't sound angry. To Shawna's surprise, she thought she heard something teasing in his voice.

"We know what happened between you. We know you got Kari's mom pregnant and somewhere, somewhere we have a brother or a sister."

Silence.

"Dad, I'm sorry we went away without telling you, but we needed to know. You wouldn't tell me and we needed to know what happened."

"You say you're with Kari Lang?" For some reason, Dad sounded grim.

"She just called her mom. And we're at her Aunt Cora's house."

"All right."

"That's all you have to say?"

Kari frowned and leaned closer.

"Just stay where you are," Dad said.

"Well." Shawna hadn't considered going anywhere else. Then again, she and Kari were making this whole thing up as they went along.

"Just promise me your crusade won't take you anywhere else."

"Okay—"

"I'm glad you called."

"Good night."

Aunt Cora was standing in the doorway when Shawna hung up the phone. Kari jumped a little, like she was surprised to see Aunt Cora, too.

"Your folks know where you are?" Aunt Cora looked at Shawna when she said that.

Shawna nodded. "Thank you for allowing us to stay over. I know it must've seemed strange to you, us showing up like this—"

"But it's really important, why we're here," Kari said. "It's something that has to do with both of us."

"Well, tell me over supper. It's not much, just meat loaf and vegetables. I wasn't expecting company."

"We're grateful for what you're doing for us." Shawna felt herself relaxing as her Lakeview Country Day School manners came back to her. How many times had she given speeches in front of the Optimists Club or the Rotary Club, seen the older white men and women smile at her with approval? It's like playing a game, her mother had said to her once. Shawna remembered it because her mother never talked much about things like race, never did or said anything to make Shawna think she was different from her schoolmates. But Mom had said one of the most useful skills she had learned in her job was the ability to make anyone feel comfortable speaking with her, by being polite and articulate, looking people in the eye. That was how she stood in front of courtrooms, stood up to high-powered people without feeling intimidated.

For the first time, Aunt Cora smiled at her. "Well, come on in and eat."

She had the kitchen table already set, and they each took a seat. Shawna wasn't looking forward to the meal, but to her surprise, the meat loaf was tasty. Shawna sat up in her chair, complimented Aunt Cora's cooking, and took good-sized portions onto her plate. She noticed Aunt Cora watching her eat.

"I've never actually seen someone eat left-handed," Aunt Cora said.

Shawna looked down at her fork. "When I was younger, I went to a summer camp in New Mexico. It was like a little finishing school. We learned how to eat continental-style and set a dinner table and waltz. Most of what we learned wasn't all that useful, but it was fun."

Kari looked impressed in a way that made Shawna uncomfortable. After all, the camp was pretty silly. "She's been all over the place," Kari said. "Traveled all over the world. She used to live in Denver."

"My parents divorced last year, and my father's from Dessina," Shawna said. "It's his hometown." She looked at

Kari, wondering how Kari knew she had traveled. She was sure they had never talked about it.

"And she's on the newspaper staff at school," Kari went on.

Aunt Cora raised her eyebrows, looking impressed. It was a look Shawna had seen before, on the faces of older white people in Dessina. It was like her accent and mannerisms contradicted the assumptions they made about black people. Maybe the Optimists and the Rotarians back in Denver looked at me like that, too, Shawna thought, and I never noticed.

"We met not too long ago." Kari's face colored a little and Shawna wondered if Kari would mention breaking the window. She didn't. "We found out our parents were—friends when they were our age."

Aunt Cora nodded slightly, without talking.

"We know that Mom spent some time here at your house—"

"And you're here wanting to know why," Aunt Cora finished for her.

Kari took a deep breath. "We think we know why."

"Why not just ask your mother?"

"She won't talk about it. So that's why we came to you. We need your help. We need to know about the baby."

Aunt Cora lowered her fork.

But Kari wouldn't back down. "Yes, we know Mom had a baby and we want to know what happened to it."

"Goodness gracious—" Aunt Cora's face reddened.

"I know people didn't talk about things like that then," Kari went on. "But see, we've got a brother or a sister somewhere and—" She looked to Shawna for help.

"And it makes all the difference in the world," Shawna said. Kari nodded in agreement.

Aunt Cora was silent for a moment. "Well, we have a lot to talk about. But I'm sure you girls are tired from your trip. You girls can sleep in the guest room tonight. I'll put towels in the bathroom. We'll talk in the morning."

"Okay," Kari said. She was smiling.

{ chapter *twenty-three* }

KARI LED THEM UP a flight of stairs to a small room that smelled a little like mothballs. There was just one double bed, covered with a white eyelet comforter. "I hope you don't steal covers," Kari said, dropping her bag on the floor.

Shawna smiled. "I don't think so."

Shawna went to the bathroom to brush her teeth and Kari snuggled under the covers. She looked around the room, taking in the wildflower wallpaper, the white nightstand and dresser with nicks in the corners, probably scraped and bumped into for years. Mom stayed in this room. Mom would have stayed here almost six months, getting bigger and bigger, sleeping every night on this bed. Kari wanted to know so many things. Did she miss Joe Riley? Write secret letters to him?

Was Mom scared when her body started changing? Was she allowed to go out much, once her condition couldn't be hidden? Kari couldn't imagine Aunt Cora as a dungeon-master. She thought that maybe Aunt Cora's face would have shown something when Kari said Shawna's name, when Kari said she knew what happened between Mom and Shawna's dad. She thought Aunt Cora's face would show some anger, or even some shock, to see the daughter of the man who almost ruined her niece. But Aunt Cora looked curious about Shawna more than anything else, curious about her speech and her manners.

The bed sank on one side as Shawna climbed in next to her. The bed immediately warmed up with the presence of another body and Kari felt toasty and comfortable.

"I was just thinking," Kari said, "wondering if Mom ever really got over your dad."

Shawna turned onto her side, facing Kari.

"I mean, they were both sent away so fast. They never got to say good-bye."

Shawna lowered her eyes, like the thought disturbed her, too. "But, come on, it was a high-school romance, right?"

"But it wasn't just ordinary high-school stuff for them. They had to be all secretive about everything. And they had a baby, which meant they were—" Kari stopped abruptly, her face hot. Shawna was smiling a little.

"It's weird to think of our parents that way," Shawna said. "Being kids like us or—" She couldn't say it, either.

Kari took a deep breath, then blurted, "Having sex?"

They both giggled, sticking their heads under the covers. It made Kari feel better that Shawna was embarrassed about it, too, that she wasn't sophisticated about everything.

"Can you imagine it?" Shawna said. "It was like Romeo and Juliet."

Kari shook her head. "No, I can't imagine it at all." She couldn't put herself inside Mom's head enough to imagine anything her mother would do.

"It's kind of romantic." Shawna turned onto her back. "It's just that—"

"What?" Kari sat up a little.

Shawna looked upset. "You read the article Marlon and Natalie wrote for the newspaper, right?"

"And now you're wondering what's gonna happen tomorrow?" Kari remembered Troy's face, red to the point of explosion, when he showed her the article. And Rick, looking at her like she had something to do with it. But the article itself, what had she thought when she read it? Nothing. She had been too surprised to think. "Troy really liked Natalie. He was gonna ask her to the ball. And the Etoiles—"

Shawna looked directly at her. "What do you think's going to happen?"

Kari was taken aback, like someone had beamed a bright light in her face. But then it came to her: When did anyone ever ask her what she thought about anything important? She turned to Shawna, adjusting the covers around her shoulders. "About Marlon and Natalie—" It just shouldn't be done; that's what Rick and Troy said in effect. What Marlon and Natalie were doing must be like trying to swim up a river flowing downstream. What would she think about it if she and Shawna hadn't learned about their parents' relationship? "I guess if they like each other—it's just that, what about the other folks who don't like it?"

"That's what I'm afraid of." Shawna sounded grim.

"I mean, our folks got sent away—"

Shawna didn't seem satisfied. "But what do you think about Marlon going to the Old South Ball with Natalie?"

Kari shook her head, not knowing what to think. "It just turns everything upside down."

"But you're going, right? To the ball?"

The ball. Just a couple of days ago, she and MC and Clare were giggling and fussing over their dresses. But she could hardly picture her dress now. It was like looking back at another person in another lifetime. "Yeah." Her voice sounded vague and uncertain.

"And if Natalie shows up at the ball with Marlon—"

"I don't know!" Kari exclaimed.

Shawna was quiet. She looked like she was somewhere deep inside herself. When she spoke again, her voice was soft. "It's like nothing's really changed. That's what makes me so scared. Your mom and my dad and now, Marlon and Natalie—"

But it looked like there was much more on her mind than what she was saying. "At your old school," Kari said, "are things different there?"

Shawna seemed to sink down into the bed, holding the covers like she wanted to pull them over her head. "I don't know."

Kari had never seen Shawna so unsure of herself, so uncertain-looking.

"All last year, I had this boyfriend, Jordan Parrish—"

"Jordan Parrish." Kari nodded, understanding immediately.

"Jordan and I went to school together since kindergarten. Everybody at school thought he was cute. But see, my old school was a lot stricter than Dessina. You couldn't kiss in the hallways. If you did, they took you to the office and gave you a warning. So it took me a while to realize he acted differently with me in public than he did in private."

Kari kept her mouth shut, willing Shawna to keep talking.

Shawna turned her back to Kari and Kari heard her sigh. "We were at the mall one day and I said something like, why are you acting so weird? He acted like he didn't know what I was talking about. But once we got to my house, he said, 'I'm afraid other people might not understand. I look at you and I see you. I don't see color.' "

"What'd your folks think?"

"Dad didn't say anything about it. I think he understood a lot more than I did and he felt sorry for me."

"And your mom?"

Shawna turned onto her back with a frown on her face. "Mom loved Jordan. She acted like everything was perfectly normal. But when we were at his house, it was like we were just friends. He said he wanted to break it to his parents slowly and I believed him."

"What about dances and stuff?"

"We'd go as friends. It wasn't until this time last year I figured everything out. You see, he didn't want to admit to anyone that he was dating a black girl."

"You think he was scared?"

"What's there to be scared of?" Shawna's voice rose. "We were in school together since kindergarten! But he was afraid to be seen with me. Like I'm something to be ashamed of."

Kari didn't know what to say.

Shawna's eyes shone in the dark, like she was about to cry. She took a deep breath and her face was full of pain. But she didn't cry.

"Maybe he really did love you," Kari said. "Maybe he was just scared."

"It doesn't make a difference."

"I guess it's more complicated than I could ever think—"

"You think people are just people."

"And now, with Marlon and Natalie," Kari began, but stopped when she saw Shawna wince. And she understood. Shawna was in love with Marlon. Kari took a deep breath. She had no idea how complicated Shawna's life was.

"I knew Marlon growing up," Shawna said. "We played together whenever I visited my grandmother. Last semester, we became great friends and I thought we had a chance."

"What do you think of Natalie?" Kari leaned forward, curious.

Shawna's face told her nothing. "I try not to think about her. Part of me hopes she truly cares about Marlon and they really like each other in spite of everything. But part of me hopes she'll flake out on him—"

"So Marlon gets taught a lesson like what happened to you?"

"That sounds so awful."

"I think that's what I'd be hoping for," Kari said. "I remember the first time I met Natalie. It was like, all of a sudden, I'm this big ugly frog standing next to a princess."

"She does look like a homecoming queen."

"Prom queen."

They both giggled, but then Shawna looked sad again and Kari turned onto her stomach, trying to think of something to say to make it all better.

"What if this is just some silly game to Natalie?" Shawna said. "And Marlon, he's got so much to lose."

"So does Natalie," Kari said. "I'll bet Troy doesn't think much of her anymore."

"You mean he's jealous?"

Kari tried to think of a way to say what she meant without offending Shawna. "There's just sort of this idea—once you date someone black—"

"I get it." Shawna sighed. "But I tell myself, just because Jordan was a creep doesn't mean everyone is. I mean, isn't that the point, not to judge everybody by what one person does?"

"I don't know if I'd have the guts," Kari said. "That's what's so weird, thinking about Mom. There's so much I don't know about her—"

"And your mom did more than just go out with my dad."

"They had a baby." But it felt good, saying that. The baby would be a grown adult now, but Kari couldn't help picturing a baby brother or sister, a tiny, cooing, laughing little thing who would make everything better. Make everything all right again.

{ chapter *twenty-four* }

SHAWNA WAS STILL ASLEEP when Kari awoke the next morning. For a few minutes, she lay in bed, warm from the sunlight pouring in from the window. Next to her, Shawna lay curled on her side, breathing lightly. Kari clasped her hands under her head. She hadn't slept so well in a long time. She smelled sausages frying down in the kitchen. It was only 8:15. The bed was warm and cozy and for a moment, Kari wondered if she should get up. How nice it would be, to lie there in a warm cocoon, feeling safe and protected. She looked at Shawna, who slept peacefully. "Everything's gonna be fine," she said. Saying it out loud made her believe it even more.

Coming back from the bathroom, she saw Shawna sitting up in bed, rubbing her eyes like she had forgotten where she was. Kari stood in the doorway. "Morning."

"Morning," Shawna said.

"I think Aunt Cora's fixed breakfast for us."

"I'll meet you downstairs."

Downstairs, Aunt Cora looked happy as well, humming to herself as she stood over the stove, flipping sausages. "Hello, sleepyhead!" she said. "Where's your friend?"

"She'll be down soon." Kari sat at the kitchen table.

Aunt Cora immediately brought her a plate of scrambled eggs and sausage. "You girls are missing school, aren't you?"

"I guess so." Kari hadn't really thought about school. "But it's important, us being here."

Aunt Cora had her back to Kari as she stood at the stove. "I reckon so."

"It's just so incredible, thinking about it," Kari said. "What happened to my mom. I keep wondering what she did while she was here."

"Read, mostly."

"I guess there wasn't much for her to do—"

"You know your mother. She wasn't one to spend time with folks," Aunt Cora said.

"No, I don't know my mother."

When Aunt Cora turned around, she looked surprised.

"I really don't," Kari insisted. "Mom's always been so quiet, never saying much about herself. And with Daddy, it's like the two of them have their own way of getting along." Aunt Cora stood there looking at her and Kari clamped her mouth shut as a flush rose on her cheeks. I'll bet that's the most Aunt Cora ever heard me say, she thought.

She took a deep breath and began speaking again. "Mom and me, we don't talk all that much. I never really noticed because of Ma Lila, you know? Ma Lila used to do all the stuff I do, like Etoiles. Mom's always busy with her patients. But then, when I found out about Mom and Shawna's dad, it made me think, there's so much I don't know about my own mother."

Aunt Cora said nothing.

"I reckon you must've been pretty shocked, finding out about Mom and Joe Riley," Kari went on. "I guess back then people didn't do things like that."

"It was a surprise, all right," Aunt Cora said.

"But you know what? Shawna has this friend at school, this black guy, and he's dating this white girl. At first it was in secret, just like Mom and Joe Riley. But now they want to be public about it. Shawna helped them get an article they wrote into our school newspaper. It's coming out today."

Aunt Cora looked deep in thought. "The world is a changing place."

"But have things really changed?" Kari said. "I mean, Shawna's all worried about what might happen to her friend once the article comes out. And the girl he's dating? She's really beautiful. Lots of guys at school like her. It makes me wonder if things have changed at all."

"Why don't you eat?" Aunt Cora motioned toward Kari's plate. "I'm keeping a plate warm for your friend."

Kari took a bite of her eggs. "What do you think of all this?"

Aunt Cora was quiet for a long time before speaking. "Y'all have a lot to learn about."

"I know," Kari said. "That's why we're here."

Shawna came into the kitchen, fully dressed. "Good morning," she said to Aunt Cora.

"Have a seat and I'll bring you a plate."

"Thank you," Shawna said as a plate of eggs and sausage was placed in front of her.

Kari leaned over the table. "Let's find out all we can about what Mom did here."

"And then maybe we can look up her doctor," Shawna said. "It might be hard, finding out what happened to the baby."

Aunt Cora joined them at the table. "Y'all are really serious about all this, aren't you?"

"Yes," Kari said. "I mean, this is our family we're talking about." But it was so much more than that. How could she explain?

Aunt Cora turned to Shawna. "Kari was just telling me about two kids writing something for the newspaper?"

Shawna looked uncomfortable. "The article comes out today."

"Kari said you were a bit nervous about it."

"We both are," Kari said. "You remember the Spring Ball? Well, Natalie wants to take Marlon as her date. No one's ever done that before."

"Everything that's happening with Marlon and Natalie made us think about what happened with our parents," Shawna said. "If things are this tense now—"

"We wonder how it was back then," Kari said. "And Mom having a baby on top of it."

"Now how did the two of you figure on a baby?" Aunt Cora asked.

"Well—" Kari took a deep breath. "Mom and Joe Riley got to be friends in the spring. Over Fourth of July, they went to the cabin up at Amicalola Falls. Then they got caught up there and Mom was sent here and Joe Riley went up to Chicago. We figured she came here right about the time she'd start to show, and she stayed until just after the baby was born."

Aunt Cora nodded slowly.

"We want to know what happened to the baby. Mom gave it up for adoption, right?"

Aunt Cora looked at the clock.

"We want to get started this morning," Shawna said. "We want to talk to Mrs. Lang's doctor if he's still here. And the adoption agency—"

"We want to find our brother or sister," Kari said. "You'll help us, won't you?"

"Y'all finished?" Aunt Cora began clearing the table. Shawna got up to help, but Aunt Cora made her sit down. "Why don't you girls go to the living room while I clean up?"

Shawna looked excited and Kari imagined she did, too. "She'll help us," Kari whispered as they went to sit in the living room. "I know she will."

The doorbell rang.

"Kari, can you answer that?" Aunt Cora called from the kitchen.

Kari shrugged and stood up. "I guess she's expecting company," she said to Shawna.

Opening the door, she came face-to-face with her mother.

{ chapter *twenty-five* }

K ARI WALKED INTO THE living room pale-faced, like someone had come up from behind and scared her. Her eyes flashed what looked like a warning, but Shawna didn't understand. Then she felt herself gasping as a blonde woman walked into the room. She looked a lot like Kari in the face. Behind the blonde woman was Dad.

"Dad?" Shawna rubbed her eye and looked again, not quite believing he was there.

"Hi, Shawna." Dad looked somber. Shawna shot Kari a look of alarm and Kari shook her head to say she didn't understand, either.

The blonde woman stood in front of Shawna and held out a hand. "I'm Allison Lang," she said. "It's nice to finally meet you, Shawna." She had a nice voice, Shawna thought. Low and mellow, with only a hint of a Southern accent. Mrs. Lang had a youngish look, making it difficult to determine her age. Looking closely, Shawna could see lines around her eyes and mouth. But with her straight blonde hair falling to her shoulders, her casual jeans, and her plaid shirt, Mrs. Lang could be Kari's older sister. Shawna couldn't imagine Mrs. Lang preening in a ball gown or gossiping with other women. She seemed like someone who would prefer her own company to the company of other people. Shawna didn't sense a driving ambition like she did with her own mother, but an aloofness that said she kept everyone around her at a distance.

Shawna swallowed. Her throat felt hot and sticky. She stood up to shake Allison Lang's hand, then sat down. "Nice to meet you, Mrs. Lang."

Mrs. Lang and Dad sat on the opposite couch. Shawna couldn't keep her head still. A quick glance out the window showed one car parked behind hers. They must have come together. Shawna looked at the clock. It was only a little after ten o'clock. They must have started out early. Shawna glanced at Kari, who was looking at her mother and Dad suspiciously. "I didn't know you were coming," Kari said.

"We had no idea what you girls were up to," Dad said. "This is some crusade."

Shawna felt sick. "Please don't joke about this."

Dad looked her in the eye. "I don't mean to joke about anything."

Kari still looked annoyed, like their parents were intruding. "Why did you come here?" She looked at her mother when she said that.

"We thought it'd be best if we talked to you girls ourselves," Dad answered.

Shawna grew angry. "But you wouldn't tell me about what happened over that Fourth of July with Kari's mom!"

"And Ma Lila, she made up some story about you having hepatitis!" Kari added.

Dad smiled. "Hepatitis?"

"We knew it was a lie."

"You both got sent away and you wouldn't say why," Shawna said.

"You concluded that I was pregnant—" Mrs. Lang began.

"It's the only thing that made sense," Shawna said. "And girls who got pregnant used to either get married or get sent away to have their babies."

"So we have a brother or sister somewhere!" Kari cut in. "That's why we're here. We want to find him and meet him and—"

"Kari," Mrs. Lang said sharply.

"You can't stop us!"

Mrs. Lang shut her eyes and breathed deeply.

"Oh, no!" Kari jumped to her feet. "You're not gonna act like this is some silly whim of mine. This is important! I know you think I don't care about anything but Etoiles and—"

"Let's not get carried away," Dad said. "That's not why we're here."

Kari sat down and Mrs. Lang opened her eyes. She looked at Kari in an odd way.

"We know it must have been really hard for you," Shawna said. "We just want to know what happened."

Mrs. Lang lowered her eyes and Shawna thought she looked upset.

"Because if we can find our brother or sister—" Kari said, impassioned.

"Kari—" Mrs. Lang cut in. "There is no brother or sister."

Shawna inhaled sharply. Kari's mouth fell open and her eyes bulged. Only Mrs. Lang and Dad's faces were unchanged as they sat calmly on the couch.

"I was never pregnant," Mrs. Lang said.

"Never pregnant?" Shawna shook her head quickly. "But Grandma Rory, she sent Dad up to Chicago and she said she prayed for him the whole way there."

"Shawna, listen to me," Dad said.

Shawna pressed her lips shut. Her chest heaved in and out, like she had to remind herself to draw breath.

"Allison and I became good friends at a time when not many black boys had friendships with white girls. From what I see going on between you kids, I guess they still don't."

"Your father and I were paired together for a project in English class," Mrs. Lang said, looking at Shawna. "I guess you can say we were both different. A lot of things important to our classmates weren't that important to us. And our school years at Dessina High were pretty tense because we were in the first integrated class to start as freshman and graduate as seniors."

"Just think of this." Dad leaned forward, looking from Kari to Shawna. "I was the only black boy in the advanced English class. When I was paired with Allison for the research project, the teacher took me aside and told me he expected me to be on my best behavior."

Shawna felt herself gasping again, but Kari sat up and exclaimed, "That's why we're here! We want to find the baby because—because—"

Mrs. Lang was looking at Kari now. "Mr. Riley and I got to be good friends while we worked on the project. Of course, I knew who he was before the project. I saw him in the hallways and sometimes we were in classes together. But there were some unwritten rules at Dessina then. Whites kept to themselves; blacks kept to themselves. That was the way it was."

Is it so different now? Shawna wondered.

"And as Mr. Riley and I got closer, yes, people at school wondered about us, talked about us. And I'll admit—" She looked at Dad and they both smiled a little, like they were sharing the same memory. "We did like each other."

"More than friends?" Shawna asked.

Dad nodded. "But we didn't want to get each other in trouble. Dessina's a small place and people were already starting to talk."

"But Fourth of July—" Shawna said.

"When we went up to my parents' cabin, we were still just friends," Mrs. Lang said. "School was out and over the summer, we would meet about once a week or so to talk. But we always had to meet secretly, and we were always afraid someone might see us. I suppose we just wanted to go away somewhere, where we wouldn't have to worry about being seen together and what might happen if we were. You know the cabin, Kari. It's quiet, out of the way. Up at Amicalola Falls, we went on long walks, hiked up the mountains—" She reached into her shirt and unfastened a necklace. Standing up, she held the necklace in front of them. Kari stood up and practically snatched it from her mother. She examined the pendant, which swung from a fine gold chain. The pendant was pinkish and rough-looking, in the shape of a triangle.

"The arrowhead?" Kari said.

"What are you talking about?" Shawna asked.

"When I saw your dad, he asked me if Mom still had the arrowhead. I didn't know what he was talking about. Later on, I asked Mom about it and she said she still had it." Kari handed the necklace back to her mother. "I've never seen you wear it, Mom."

Mrs. Lang didn't respond to that. Instead, she said, "We found it while we were hiking near the waterfall. It was a wonderful weekend until Sunday morning—" She looked at Dad.

"Allison's brother showed up Sunday morning." Dad's face still looked composed, but his mouth was pressed tight when he spoke. "And when he saw us at the cabin together, all kinds of accusations flew. When we got back to Dessina, your grandmother thought it would be best to pack me up and send me to Chicago."

Kari looked sick. "Because you didn't know what Uncle Robert would do? Or my grandfather?"

Dad let silence fill the room and Shawna felt the tension pressing down on all of them. Mrs. Lang stared at her hands, clasped tightly in her lap. Kari's nose wrinkled, like a noxious odor had filled the room. Shawna felt herself breathing quickly.

"Dessina's a strange place in many ways," Dad said finally. "Life seems to go on as it has for decades, but at the same time, change is occurring so slowly, you don't see it happening. And then, something happens that makes you realize things have changed."

Kari looked as confused as Shawna felt.

"Your grandmother." Dad was looking at Shawna now. "She couldn't consider the possibility that times had changed in Dessina by nineteen seventy-one. All she could think about was what would have happened to me twenty years before that."

"I don't understand!" Kari cried out.

"That's what I mean about Dessina being a strange place. The world is still turning, although sometimes you wouldn't know it. Looking back now, I don't believe I would have come to some bad end if I hadn't gone to Chicago. People in Dessina would have talked, and to a certain extent, both Allison and I would've been ostracized. But I believe that would have been all."

Mrs. Lang's voice was soft when she spoke. "My brother and my mother were very angry when I came back from Amicalola Falls. My mother was afraid for my reputation in Dessina. So that's why I came here to Knoxville."

"I don't get it," Shawna said. "Why didn't you just run away?"

Dad laughed, but it didn't sound like he was making fun of her. "You girls are brave, probably a lot braver than we were. And don't forget, Shawna, you're a lot more worldly than I ever was. When I went to Chicago, that was only the second time I'd ever been out of Georgia."

"Your father and I didn't stop communicating when we left Dessina," Mrs. Lang said. "In the letters I got from him, he said he was happy in Chicago. Happy to be in a big city."

"Two weeks after I arrived in Chicago, my mother called me to ask if I wanted to come home," Dad said. "I told her I wanted to stay in Chicago. Just like you girls, I was learning what it meant to be independent, to make a life of my own."

"And me, I was happy to be away from my mother," Mrs. Lang said. "Living here with Aunt Cora was a pleasant experience for me. Aunt Cora didn't fuss over me or try to push me into a lifestyle I didn't want."

"But you came back in January—" Kari said.

"Because my father got sick," Mrs. Lang said. "After what happened over the summer, I never thought I'd go home again. But then, with my father ill, I learned something important. The people you love may disappoint you, but you can't turn your back on them."

Kari shook her head. "I don't believe you."

"What?" Dad asked.

"I think you're lying. I think you just don't want to tell us about the baby! Maybe you're scared we're gonna find it!"

"Kari—" Shawna began.

"We are!" Kari stood up, raising her voice. "We're gonna find out the truth! So go home if you don't want to help us! Just go home!" But Kari sank onto the couch and put her hands over her face. Her shoulders shook and Shawna could hear the sobs escaping from behind her hands.

"Kari," Shawna whispered, but she felt the energy draining from her body. So we were wrong, she thought. It made her feel empty, thinking about that. Like all the emotion churning inside her had suddenly gone flat.

Dad and Mrs. Lang looked at each other like they didn't know what to do.

"Just go away, all of you," Kari said without moving her hands.

Watching Kari cry, Shawna didn't know what to do either, how to fill the emptiness inside of her. Dad and Mrs. Lang sat there, but nobody said anything. There was nothing more to say.

{ chapter *twenty-six* }

KARI COULDN'T SPEAK. She had stopped crying over an hour ago. She sat looking out the window, staring down at the pools of water at the base of the Smoky Mountains. They would be in Georgia soon. Then it would be back home to Dessina.

Mom was driving, and she had said nothing since the start of the trip. What a horrible, horrible morning, Kari thought. Looking in the side mirror, she saw two red-stained eyes staring back at her from a blotchy, red face. She leaned against the door, squeezing her eyes shut.

No brother or sister. It was like a cruel joke.

Saying good-bye had been awkward. Kari and Shawna went upstairs to pack their things, neither of them saying anything. Mom had thanked Aunt Cora for taking care of them.

And then Shawna and Joe Riley left in Shawna's car. Kari and Shawna didn't even look at each other as they were leaving. But what could they possibly say after everything that had happened? Mom and Joe Riley had come in just when Kari thought she was taking charge of things, about to discover something on her own. All of a sudden, they were the adults and Kari and Shawna were two silly girls who had figured everything wrong.

Mom had tried talking to Kari as they drove out of Knoxville. "It seems like you girls are really disappointed," Mom said, but Kari clamped her hands over her ears. Thinking about that now made her feel stupid. It was a childish thing to do, but Kari didn't want to hear Mom say she felt sorry for her or for Mom to tell her, "That's what happens when you act before you know the truth." Stick to the Etoile Club, Kari could imagine Mom saying. That's all you're good for.

She felt sobs rising again, but she held them down the best she could. She didn't want to cry in front of her mother. It was easier just to be angry. She turned to glare at Mom, who must have seen from the corner of her eye because her hands twitched on the steering wheel.

"It seems like you have a lot you want to say to me," Mom said.

"I don't have anything to say to you." Kari pressed her arms tighter against her chest.

"I'm sorry you're so upset."

"You don't get it!" Kari cried out. She choked on a sob, then swallowed it down.

"Why don't you help me understand, then?"

Kari slumped in her seat. "Like you've ever cared about anything I do."

"Where is this coming from?"

"Turning your nose up at everything I do, like I'm some stupid idiot—" Kari felt hot tears on her face. "I was thinking, if you had a baby, then maybe I could understand it. Why you always seem like you're someplace else. But now, I don't know!"

Mom said nothing.

"Why did you come back to Dessina, anyway? Why didn't you just stay away?"

Mom made a sharp right turn into a service station.

"What are we stopping for?" Kari asked.

"We need gas." Mom got out of the car, her face expressionless. They could have been talking about the weather.

Returning to the car, Mom stuck the key into the ignition, but she didn't turn it. For a moment, she just sat there.

"I hate you," Kari said.

Mom looked up sharply, her eyes startled-looking. But then she turned to face forward and started the ignition.

Kari unlocked the door and got out of the car. She started walking toward the road without looking back. She just walked, not thinking, not wondering where she was going. She put her hands into the pockets of her jeans and lengthened her stride.

A car pulled up behind her but she ignored it, walking onto the shoulder of the road. But then she heard her name. "Kari!" Mom's voice was sharp and full of anger.

"I'm not going anywhere with you," Kari said without looking back.

"Kari, get in the car."

The shoulder was smooth and straight and it felt nice to walk. Kari felt herself breaking into an easy jog. The sun warmed the top of her head and the wind was cool on her face. She ran faster, down a steep incline. Her legs cut through the wind and her arms pumped at her sides. She wasn't thinking. She was just feeling and doing and she was happy, just like she was when she woke up this morning next to Shawna. Like everything was all right in the world and all she had to do was get up and enjoy it.

Her foot caught on something and she felt a sharp, twisting pain as her legs collapsed underneath her. "Damn it!" Kari said through clenched teeth. She reached down for her ankle and sharp pains shot through her lower leg. She shut her eyes tightly.

A car pulled to a stop behind her, and Kari soon heard approaching footsteps. "Move your hand." Mom knelt beside her and began probing the ankle with her fingers.

"Ow!"

"Nothing's broken," Mom said. "It's probably a slight sprain. Come on, I'll help you to the car."

With a grimace, Kari pulled herself to her feet. She tried putting weight on her right leg, but it almost buckled underneath her from the pain.

"I'll help you," Mom said again. She sounded impatient. Kari looked at her suspiciously, then began hopping toward the car on one leg. Gritting her teeth, Kari opened the door, then fell onto the front seat, pushing it back as far as it would go and stretching her right leg in front of her.

Mom shut the door behind her, then walked around to the driver's side. As Mom got into the car, Kari steeled herself for a barrage of questions. Why do a stupid thing like that? or maybe, What have I ever done to you?

But Mom didn't say anything. She kept checking the mirrors, waiting for the interstate to clear before she pulled onto the road. The car coasted downhill, toward the Georgia state line. Fine lines appeared around Mom's mouth, like she was pressing her lips tight, holding something in. She must hate me, Kari thought, for saying I hated her. It made her feel numb, thinking about it.

Mom's eyelashes darkened and Kari saw a single tear trickle down Mom's face. Mom reached up to touch it, then wiped it from her cheek. Kari frowned. Had she ever seen Mom cry before? Mom's lips trembled. She kept reaching up and wiping away the tears rolling down her face, but she didn't make a sound.

Kari faced forward, her own face heating up. But no tears came. Her ankle throbbed whenever she moved it. She jiggled her foot, sending a constant flow of pain through her ankle.

"I'll set your ankle when we get home." Mom's voice was steady when she spoke.

"All right," Kari said. A sign, **DESSINA 45**, whizzed past. They were almost home.

❦ chapter *twenty-seven* ❧

G RANDMA RORY WAS WAITING for them in the living room as Shawna and her father walked in the door. Shawna immediately fell onto the sofa. Dad took off his shoes, weary-eyed.

"I thought y'all might want a late lunch," Grandma Rory said. "I fixed some chicken."

"Thanks, but I'm not hungry." Shawna closed her eyes, exhausted. So much had happened today and it was only midafternoon.

"I'll save it for dinner, then."

Shawna checked her watch. School would just be getting out. Going to school tomorrow, facing Troy and Kessler in newspaper class, seeing Marlon and Natalie, it was too much to think about.

She thought Dad might go about his business, go upstairs, or maybe go out to the basketball court with his friends. Instead, he sat with her on the couch.

"Ready to talk now?" he asked.

Shawna shrugged and sat up to make more room for him. They hadn't spoken during the drive home. Dad had tried talking to her, but Shawna had just turned away and stared at the passing scenery. It hurt to talk, or even to think. She felt like a gaping hole had opened in her chest, draining out all her feelings. She wondered why she didn't get upset, like Kari. Kari was practically in hysterics before they left. Shawna could hardly look at her. Still, she couldn't remember when she had ever felt a loss so deeply. Even her parents telling her they were getting divorced last summer didn't hurt like this. She had been sad, yes. Sad and hurt and angry. But it wasn't like she hadn't seen it coming. And when Dad said he wanted to go back to Dessina, Shawna realized that she could go, too. She could start life all over again at a new school.

She looked up at last year's school picture, hanging on the wall opposite her. But what have I come to now? she wondered. Was she any better off now than she was in Denver?

Dad hadn't said anything. He was looking at her in a way Shawna had never seen him look at her before. It was like he was realizing she was a different person, that there was much more to her than he had realized.

"Dad?" Shawna cleared her throat. "Why did you want to come back here?"

Dad looked around the room before he answered, his eyes stopping on different objects: couches, photographs, and knickknacks that had probably been here since he was a boy. "To Dessina?" he said. "Maybe it's the way that you can turn around and look out over the valley when you reach the top of

Old Dessina Road. Or maybe it's the way I can meet up with the boys I grew up with on the basketball court and that we can all talk about the families we have now. Or maybe it's knowing that your grandmother grew up in this house and that her grandmother and grandfather built it up from a two-room cabin. Maybe it's knowing that five generations of this family have lived in this house, built their lives here."

"But what about our house in Denver?"

Dad looked sad when he spoke. "The house you grew up in was nice, wasn't it?"

"Yeah—"

"But to me, it could have been any nice house in any suburb of any city. Our neighbors moved in and out every few years. That's not what I wanted from life."

"What do you want?"

"To grow old here. I may not like everything I see here, but I understand this place. I know it intimately. It's a part of me."

Shawna sighed. "I've never felt that way about anywhere."

"And that's one of the biggest regrets I have."

Shawna felt herself sniffling and suddenly, she was in Dad's arms. But she wasn't a little girl again, protected and content. Leaning against Dad's shoulder, feeling the soft cotton of his shirt under her cheek, she only felt sadder.

"But what if things had been different?" she asked. "What if you and Mrs. Lang could have really gotten together?"

"We could have. Looking back now, I think that neither one of us really had the courage to stand up to everyone and say what we felt."

"Are you still in love with her?" She looked up at Dad's face, expecting to see a sad expression.

Instead, Dad chuckled. "When you're young, you feel a lot

of things. But a lot of what you're feeling is youth itself. Do you understand that?"

"I don't know."

"You want to know if I still wonder what could have been, what might have been?" Dad sighed. "It's romantic and it's pretty to think that I would, but the truth is, I don't. I went to college, I got my teaching certificate, I got married, I had you. And Allison Craighead became a fond memory. That's how life works. Life is about people coming and going all the way through."

Dad squeezed her close. "We think sometimes that every person we care about, we can hold close to us forever. But we can't. And that's what makes our memories so special."

Shawna closed her eyes and breathed deeply. She was shaking a little. She felt like crying but she wasn't sure why.

"We wanted it so much." Her voice was unsteady. "I didn't know how much I wanted there to be a brother or a sister—"

"I know." Dad's voice was soothing. "It broke my heart, seeing Kari Lang crying like that. I could tell how much this meant to you."

"I haven't told you about what's going on at school," Shawna said. "Marlon, he's been dating this girl, Natalie. She's white. And this week, instead of my column, I put an article they wrote in its place. They wrote about being together, how they don't want to hide it anymore."

"Oh, Shawna."

"They want to go to the Old South Ball together, if you can believe it. I guess Natalie really liked the article I wrote about it and she wants to take Marlon as her date. The newspaper came out today."

"And you have no idea what happened?"

"I don't even know what to think! I always hoped that Marlon—" She couldn't say any more, or else she really would cry.

Dad was stroking her shoulder. "I know you must be disappointed."

"Especially after Jordan." Shawna felt tears welling in her eyes. "Is anybody ever gonna think I'm good enough?"

"Don't you ever think like that!" Dad's voice was fierce and he held her tight. "You are a beautiful, talented, and courageous young woman! I won't let one cowardly boy let you feel bad about yourself! I won't do it!" Dad sounded like he was about to cry, too.

"I try not to," Shawna managed to say. "But now, Marlon with Natalie—"

Dad didn't answer.

"But what if he just likes her blonde hair?"

"You don't know one way or the other."

Shawna hiccuped and sat up straight. "What about you and Allison? Did you like her blonde hair?"

"Allison was my friend," Dad said. "We talked about all kinds of things, our dreams, what we wanted from life. You want to know if I was attracted to her? Sure I was. Just like she was attracted to me. But you want to know if it was because of or in spite of the fact she was white? It's not that simple, really."

"I guess not—"

"Forbidden fruit is tempting," Dad said. "I'd be lying if I said it wasn't. But when you're talking about a good friend, it's the relationship you have that's important."

Shawna stared at the floor.

"You've been lonely here. I know that."

"I'd feel this way in Denver, too. It's just that there, it's easier to pretend."

"So what are you going to do about it?"

"I don't know," Shawna said. "I guess I'll have to keep trying to make friends who'll like me for who I am. I mean, I'm really not weird or stuck up, am I?"

Dad's eyes were shiny as he shook his head. "Of course not."

As she leaned into Dad's shoulder again, Shawna saw Grandma Rory watching them from the hallway. She must have overheard everything they said. Her arms were crossed and she was nodding as if to say she approved. And she was proud.

{ chapter *twenty-eight* }

MOM WRAPPED KARI'S ANKLE with an Ace bandage, then told Kari to lie on the couch with her leg elevated. She left the room and came back with an ice pack. "It'll keep the swelling down."

"Thanks," Kari muttered, balancing the ice pack on her ankle.

Mom sat next to her on the couch with her hands folded in her lap. She sat there without saying anything, making Kari feel uncomfortable.

"What?" Kari snapped.

"Do you want to talk?"

Kari lowered her eyes to her leg, stretched out in front of her on the couch. She couldn't think of anything to say. So she picked up the remote control and flipped on the television, hoping Mom would get the message.

She did. Mom got up and left the room without another word. Kari was glad. She scanned the channels quickly, but there was nothing she wanted to look at so she turned off the television and looked around the den. A few school pictures of Kari were propped on an end table and she glanced over them quickly. One family picture hung on the wall, taken five years ago. They hadn't taken a family picture since then. Kari didn't think it was a very good picture. Only Daddy looked good, smiling in his normal, easy way. Mom looked a little bit impatient in the picture, like she wanted to get the whole thing over with as soon as possible. And Kari? She sat in front of them, leaning against Daddy's chest. She thought her smile looked stupid. Fake. But looking at the picture, she wished Daddy was here now and that she could snuggle up with him, like a little girl. But you're not a little girl, Kari told herself. And Daddy wouldn't be able to take the pain away.

Kari was trying to shut them out, but all of the events of the day kept intruding in her mind. The morning had started so promisingly, so full of hope. Who would've thought after all that I'd end up here in my own house, she thought, not able to move on account of a sprained ankle? She thought about reading something, but she didn't have the energy to get up and find a book.

Thankfully, Ma Lila was out. Kari cringed at the thought of talking to Ma Lila, explaining where she had been last night. It would be like finding herself stuck in a room with Jolie and Kessler, unable to escape. Ma Lila sent Mom away because she was afraid of what all the Jolies and Kesslers of the world would think about Mom being friends with Joe Riley. Thinking about the Etoiles brought a bad taste to her mouth, but the bad taste soon faded to nothing. No brother, no sister. No connection with Shawna. Shawna left this morning without a word. Your friend, Aunt Cora called her. But what reason did they have to be friends now? Her ankle hurt and she reached under the cold ice to rub it. The skin felt numb and disconnected.

The doorbell rang and Kari felt herself tensing. She heard footsteps, presumably Mom, going to the door. Then she heard heavier footsteps growing louder until someone entered the den.

When she looked up, she saw Rick, who immediately came to kneel beside her. "Kari!" He sounded worried.

Kari glanced at the clock. It was just after two-thirty; school would have just gotten out. "Don't you have practice?"

"I wanted to come by and make sure you were all right."

Kari looked him up and down. She felt irritated but she wasn't sure why.

Rick put his arms around her and Kari stiffened as her head touched his chest. She pulled away, leaning her face against the sofa.

He was looking at her leg. "What happened to your ankle?"

"Sprained it."

"Where have you been? Your grandma called me, looking for you—"

Kari studied his face as he talked, the sandy blond hair curling around his ears. He had a nice tan from spending so much time outside. Did he always have that small brown mole next to his nose? Did his eyebrows always look scruffy?

"Have you been listening?" Rick asked.

"No."

He looked surprised, then he squinted like he was trying to bring her into sharper focus. "The newspaper came out to-day." Rick sounded impatient, like he was repeating himself.

Kari's ears perked with interest. "What happened?"

Rick shrugged. "I didn't see Natalie or Marlon in the halls, but Troy did. He's so mad, he can hardly look either one of them in the face without wanting to—" He cut himself off sharply. "I still can't believe Marlon and Shawna did that—"

"I don't want to talk about that!" Kari snapped.

"You went somewhere with her, didn't you?"

Kari didn't answer. She could feel herself frowning.

"I talked to Clare and she said you left the Etoile meeting to go somewhere with Shawna."

"It was a stupid meeting, anyway," Kari muttered. "All they did was kick Natalie out."

"But where did y'all go?"

Kari said nothing.

Rick looked angry. "Why won't you tell me about it?"

"I just don't want to talk about it." Kari shut her eyes, hoping he would get the point. And with her eyes shut, her mind felt heavy and fatigued.

"Kari, why won't you talk to me?" Rick raised his voice, which irritated Kari even more. Didn't he know she could hear him just fine?

"Why don't you just go to practice?"

"No, I wanna talk to you. I wanna know what's going on with you. Kari—" His hands were on her shoulders and he turned them sharply, so that she had no choice but to look at him.

"Let go of me!" Kari shook him off and scooted as far back onto the couch as she could. She must have been glaring at him because he was glaring back, his shoulders heaving.

"This's what I get, huh?" he exclaimed. "For trying to show you I love you? What'd I do to you, huh?"

The word *love* made Kari wince. She leaned her cheek against the rough upholstery. What's wrong with me? she asked herself. Why does everything just feel so bad?

"Kari." Rick's voice was tender, and she felt his fingers smoothing her hair. But his touch only made everything worse. Nothing could fill it, the hollow ache inside of her.

"Please go." Her voice was barely a whisper. "I just want to be by myself right now."

"But—"

"Go!" Kari sat up and turned on him. "Leave me alone!"

Rick sat where he was, dazed-looking, like someone had hit him. But the look on his face only made Kari angrier.

"I said go!" To make her point, she shoved him away from her as hard as she could.

But Rick stayed right where he was, his mouth hanging open like Kari had metamorphosed into someone else right in front of him.

"And I don't want to go to the prom and I don't want to go to that stupid ball!" Kari said. "So find someone else to take."

"What?" Rick's face reddened and the cords of his neck tightened. He narrowed his eyes at her. She'd never seen him look so angry. Part of her wanted to take it back, take back everything she had said, fall against Rick and let him hold her. Tell him she was sorry.

"Just go," Kari said. She felt sick. She couldn't say all of that. She couldn't say anything, so she turned her back to Rick, burying her face in the sofa.

"But you love me!" Rick's voice cracked.

Kari didn't turn around. She didn't have anything else to say.

She heard him leaving. She heard the front door slam and, listening hard, she heard his car engine start, the sound fading as he drove away. She wondered if Mom heard any of that. She wasn't sure if she knew what Mom really thought of Rick, anyway. Daddy loved him, Ma Lila loved him, but Mom treated him with the same cool respect that she treated everybody.

You shouldn't have been so mean, she told herself. Rick didn't deserve that. Nothing that happened was his fault. But she couldn't make herself get up off the couch, go after him.

But you love me, Rick had said. She had always said she did, hadn't she? But now she didn't know. She didn't know about anything anymore.

Her eyes spilled weak tears that she could barely feel on her face. "I'm sorry—" she whispered. But there was no one to hear her say it.

{ chapter *twenty-nine* }

RIVING TO SCHOOL WEDNESDAY morning, Shawna tried to get herself back into the mode of school life. Prom was this Saturday, but she wasn't going. She had no one to go with.

The hallways were empty and Shawna was glad. The students wouldn't arrive for another twenty minutes or so. She had some time to pull herself together, to get ready to face the day.

She hadn't called Marlon last night, even though she thought about him for a long time before she fell asleep. She was dying to know what had happened at school on Tuesday, but she couldn't bring herself to call him. It's his problem, she finally told herself. His and Natalie's. She didn't have the strength to take it on as her own.

The light was on in Mrs. Richter's classroom and Shawna held her head a little higher as she approached. Would Marlon be here? Would Mrs. Richter get mad at her for sneaking Marlon's editorial into the newspaper?

Marlon was there. He sat by himself near the back of the room, looking through a stack of photographs. Troy and Kessler whispered to each other. They looked up as Shawna walked in. She could see them from the corner of her eye, even though she had her eyes on Marlon.

"Where were you yesterday?" Marlon asked as she sat next to him.

"It's a long story."

"I came by last night but your dad said you were asleep." He spoke in a low voice, so that Kessler and Troy wouldn't be able to hear.

"I was," Shawna said. "I went to bed at eight o'clock. I had a tough day."

Marlon leaned forward like he expected her to tell him about it. Shawna kept her mouth shut.

"Are you okay?" he asked.

Shawna stared at a desk and sighed. "I don't know."

"Kessler said yesterday that you showed up at their Etoile meeting or whatever and took Kari Lang away with you. Isn't that the girl who broke your window?"

Shawna laughed. Kari never did say why she did that. She remembered Dad saying that maybe Kari was jealous. It was strange, to think a girl like Kari, with a boyfriend and popularity, would be jealous of Shawna. But after everything that happened yesterday, maybe it wasn't so strange after all.

"Shawna—"

Shawna blinked rapidly and looked up. "What?"

"You went somewhere with Kari Lang?"

"Yes, but I don't want to talk about that now. Tell me what happened yesterday."

Marlon looked somber. "There was all kinds of hell raised in newspaper yesterday. I just sat here while Troy and Kessler hollered. Talking about journalistic integrity and I had no right to do what I did and you were using the newspaper to advance your own agenda, blah blah blah—"

Shawna shrugged. "Some of that's probably true."

"But since when do they get all sanctimonious?" Marlon said. "I think you're the best thing that's ever happened to this news rag."

"You do?"

"Well, yeah. And I'm not even talking about the ball. You're not afraid to stand up to folks, say what you think. I think that's why Natalie wanted to write that article in the first place. I think she really likes you."

"She likes me?" Shawna was astounded. When had she ever been friendly to Natalie? It must have shown, her anger and, she could admit it, her jealousy.

"I want you to get to know her. There's more to her than you think."

Shawna felt guilty. "Marlon, if you guys are happy—"

Marlon reached across his desk and took her hand. "I know lots more than you think I do. I know what you were thinking about me."

Shawna took a deep breath and held it in. I will not cry, she told herself.

"When you moved here, I was so glad. Finally, there was someone here who wasn't stuck thinking this is nineteen sixty-three or something. You've been places, done stuff most people around here don't even dream about."

Shawna couldn't speak.

"I thought about you the same way. I don't know; maybe I was scared. I like being friends with you, knowing I can talk to you about anything. I don't know; sometimes people lose that when they start going out together. And then, I'm not even sure if I know how to be a good boyfriend and maybe I'd mess things up—"

Shawna was crying. She couldn't help it. She wasn't crying loudly enough for anyone else to hear, but the tears rolled down her face and she couldn't stop them.

"Hey, I didn't mean to make you upset—" Marlon pulled his chair next to her and put an arm around her shoulders. Troy and Kessler must be looking at us, she thought, but it didn't matter. Marlon gave her a handkerchief and she wiped her face, then blew her nose.

"I shouldn't have gone into all that here," he whispered.

"Doesn't matter," Shawna choked out. She shrugged off Marlon's arm and took deep breaths to stop herself from crying.

"Yes, I want to get to know Natalie," she said, hiccuping. "If she's your friend, she'll be my friend, too."

"I never meant for anything to happen between me and Natalie," Marlon said. "But it did and I want you to understand about it."

Looking up, Shawna saw Troy looking at her, puzzled. He didn't look like he was gloating, even though she knew her nose was red and her eyes swollen from crying. In fact, he looked a little sad, like maybe he understood.

Mrs. Richter rushed into the room fifteen minutes before the first bell. She looked at Shawna gravely but said nothing. She went straight to Troy, who was asking her something about a news story.

"I wonder if she's mad at me," Shawna said.

"Doubt it."

"I guess I should get to work. I have to write a column for next week."

Her editorial staff members were starting to drift into the room, along with the other newspaper staffers. But Shawna didn't feel like working. She didn't feel like being at school.

One of Marlon's sports staffers, Tameka Wood, rushed into the room. She was a tall, light-skinned girl who played on the freshman basketball team. Shawna didn't know her that well. Tameka's chest heaved, like she had been running down the hallway. She went straight to Marlon. "I think you better come with me."

Marlon stood up. "What?"

Tameka looked uncomfortable. "It's about a—friend of yours."

Marlon looked at Mrs. Richter. "Can we be excused?"

"The bell hasn't rung yet," she said, "but if you're late, I won't mark you tardy."

Marlon and Shawna followed Tameka out of the room. Once they were outside, Tameka turned to Marlon. "It's your girlfriend," she said. The word *girlfriend* fell out of her mouth like she had to force it out.

Marlon looked frightened. "What?"

"I was coming into the building and I saw her coming in, too. And then this group of girls, they came up behind her and kind of pushed her over by the flagpole and—"

Shawna sucked in her breath.

"Somebody went to get an administrator and it got broke up real fast. She's in the nurse's office—"

Marlon took off down the hallway with Shawna and Tameka at his heels. He tore through the front office to the student clinic. A nurse met him at the door.

"Natalie—" he said.

"Over there." The nurse stepped aside and Shawna saw Natalie sitting doubled over on the bed, sobbing.

"Natalie—" Marlon kneeled in front of her and lifted her face by the chin. Natalie's left eye looked swollen and the skin around it bruised to a deep purple. Her lips were purple and swollen as well. Marlon sat on the bed, wrapping his arms around Natalie's shoulders and pulling her face to his chest. Shawna felt a flash of envy as Marlon rubbed her back, but it disappeared when she saw Marlon's face, his jaw taut with anger.

"It's all right," he whispered to her.

"Natalie?" Shawna spoke softly. "What happened?"

Natalie hiccuped. She was trembling, even with Marlon's strong fingers stroking her hair. "I was walking in and—these girls—I don't know them—they come up to me and say, oh, you think you're all of that? You—you think you can be sweet on Marlon, white bitch? And then they . . . they start hitting me and—"

Marlon held her face by the chin and studied her bruises. "What'd the nurse say?"

"She says I'm okay, but she's excusing me for the rest of the day." Again, she hiccuped. "Can you take me home?"

"Yeah, of course I'll take you home." Marlon met eyes with Shawna.

"I'll tell Mrs. Richter," Shawna said. "I'm sorry about what happened, Natalie."

Natalie didn't say anything. She was still trembling and crying.

Shawna backed out of the room, almost running into Tameka. She forgot Tameka was there. Tameka leaned in the doorway, her arms crossed as she watched Marlon with Natalie, expressionless.

Shawna left the clinic and fell into the crowd in the hall-way. The din of students talking and laughing swirled around her. She went to her locker, where Sephora sat on the floor with Tashi, the two of them comparing class notes.

"Shawna!" Sephora called to her. Shawna sat down with them and felt Tashi eyeing her, those well-manicured eyebrows lifted as she looked Shawna up and down. Stop it, Shawna wanted to say to her, but Sephora stuck a Dum Dum sucker in front of her.

"No, thanks." Shawna waved it away and Sephora stuck it in her pocket.

"You missed one crazy day yesterday!" Sephora said. "Did you know about Marlon and some white girl? I almost fell out when I read about it in the newspaper. I couldn't believe it!"

"Marlon's girlfriend got beat up this morning." Shawna's voice sounded flat and lifeless. She had been so busy worrying about Marlon, she never thought to worry about Natalie.

Sephora's eyes grew round. "For real?"

"I just saw her. She looks really bad."

Tashi's narrow shoulders rose and fell. "Well, what does she expect? We'll all be reaching out to her with open arms?"

"But—"

Sephora shrugged as well. "I don't feel sorry for her, ei-ther."

"But it's between Marlon and Natalie!" Shawna exclaimed.

Tashi shook her head. "Maybe it's different where you come from. But I thought after reading that stupid article yes-terday, that was the last we'd see of Marlon. That some of these crackers here would finish him off."

"Well, it's Natalie who got beat up," Shawna said.

Sephora smiled a little. "Chickens coming home to roost."

Tashi leaned forward. "Marlon knows better than that. If

he thinks he can show up at the Cracker Ball, he is one stupid idiot."

"Shoot, girl, if anybody should be mad at Marlon, it's you!" Sephora took the sucker from her mouth and pointed it at Shawna. "He's been stringing you along all this time and then some white thing comes swishing up to him and he's gone—"

"It's not like that—" Shawna's voice was faint.

Neither Tashi nor Sephora said anything else. They returned to their notes and Shawna stood up. The first bell was about to ring, anyway. She left without saying good-bye, her eyes fixed on the orange carpet.

Turning the corner, she nearly ran straight into Kari Lang.

They both stopped and looked at each other. Kari leaned on a pair of crutches and Shawna looked down to see her foot wrapped in a bandage.

"Sprained my ankle," Kari said before Shawna could ask.

"That's too bad." But it was strange, seeing Kari now. Kari had deep circles under her eyes, like she hadn't slept. Instead of her usually fussy skirts and tops, she wore sweat pants and a sloppy T-shirt, her hair tied loosely into a ponytail.

They looked at each other and Shawna wished she could think of something to say. She smiled a little, and Kari smiled, too. And then the bell rang and they continued on in opposite directions.

{ chapter *thirty* }

KARI LIMPED DOWN THE hallway on her crutches, keeping her eyes on the ground. She took a different route to algebra class to avoid MC and Clare. This morning she rode the bus to school. It had been strange, standing there at the bus stop with the freshmen and sophomores she'd never before paid any attention to. But she didn't want to hear MC and Clare's questions or hear them talk about the ball. So far, she had managed to avoid Rick as well.

She still felt bad about how she had treated him last night, how mean she had been. She had thought about calling him, saying she was sorry. But *what would I have said?* she thought as she hobbled toward her next class. *What would I have said if he told me he loved me?* The thought made her cringe, made her feel irritated and sad at the same time.

But seeing Shawna, she didn't know what to think. Shawna had smiled, but things were different now. All through algebra and English class, Kari stared at her notebook, not paying attention. By lunchtime, she was ready to go home. She thought about going to the nurse's office, saying her ankle hurt too much. Maybe she could be excused for the day. She could call Mom and ask to be picked up. But she and Mom still weren't talking.

On her way to the office, she saw MC and Clare. There was no way to avoid them; they were rushing toward her. Kari stood where she was.

They both looked really nice. MC's hair was in a French braid, lying neatly against her back, and she wore a floral minidress she had bought on their trip to Atlanta. Clare's blonde hair poufed around her face, her clothes a careful imitation of MC's.

"Kari!" Clare sounded upset. "Why are you avoiding us?"

MC looked at her crutches. "What happened to you?"

"Sprained my ankle," Kari said. They were blocking her path and she felt edgy. "I'm gonna go to the nurse and see if she'll let me go home."

"I'll take you home," MC said firmly. "Then your mom can call the attendance office."

"I don't know—"

"Something's got you upset." MC sounded angry. "But why are you mad at us?"

Clare was near tears. "What did we do?"

Kari said nothing.

"Rick called me last night," MC said. "He said you broke up with him."

Kari blinked at that. Had she broken up with him? "I guess I did."

"But why?" Clare exclaimed.

Kari didn't answer. She felt MC and Clare looking at her suspiciously. Suddenly, she felt exhausted. She slumped a little on her crutches.

"I'll drive you home." MC took off Kari's backpack and slung it over her shoulder. Having no choice, Kari followed them out of the building, leaning on her crutches.

"Wait here and I'll get the car," MC said, leaving Kari and Clare in front of the building.

Kari watched MC walking toward the parking lot.

"I don't get it," Clare said. "We were all so happy last weekend. What's different now?"

Kari lowered her eyes to the pavement, wishing she hadn't come to school at all. It was too soon to try to explain things to Clare and MC. She needed more time to herself.

MC pulled up in front of the school. Clare climbed into the backseat and Kari sat up front, resting her crutches on her leg.

MC lit a cigarette.

"You're just gonna have to quit someday," Kari muttered.

MC shrugged. "Maybe so."

Kari listened to the engine humming as MC drove through downtown Dessina, then down the hill of Old Dessina Road.

Clare was crying. Kari heard her sniffling in the backseat. MC dragged on her cigarette, flicking the ashes out the window.

"The meeting ended after you left," MC said. "Nobody knew what to say after that."

Kari half nodded and half shrugged.

"And I heard something in English class," MC went on. "That girl Natalie, she got beat up by a couple of black girls this morning."

Kari looked up quickly. "What?"

"She's okay, though. She got sent home."

"Oh, no—" Kari immediately thought of Shawna.

MC pulled over onto the side of the road and cut off the engine. In the backseat, Clare continued to sob. Kari felt her arms and legs tensing. Her ankle ached.

"What?" she said finally.

MC turned to look at her and Kari thought she saw a hint of sadness in MC's face. "Shawna seemed out of it in class today. I figured whatever was up with her's up with you, too."

Kari didn't answer.

"Aren't we best friends?" Clare cried from the backseat. "What did we do wrong?"

Kari leaned against the window. "It's not you. It's me. And some of it's Shawna, too."

"Has she been trying to turn you against us?" Clare shot out.

Kari turned around to look at Clare's tear-streaked face. She thought she'd be angry, or at least annoyed, to see Clare so upset, but she wasn't.

"It's nothing like that," Kari said softly. "You see—" Before she knew it, she was telling them the whole story. She told them about her mom and Shawna's dad, and how they thought they might have a brother or sister between them. She watched MC's face pique with interest and Clare's go blank with confusion. She told them about the trip to Tennessee.

"My goodness." MC stubbed out her cigarette.

"But what about Rick?" Clare asked.

Kari sighed. "I was in a bad mood when he came over. It's just that—" She stopped. How could she explain to them that she felt like she was changing? That she wasn't sure who she was anymore or what she wanted?

MC restarted the car. "Want me to pick you up before the meeting?"

"Meeting?" Kari said, confused. But then she remembered. Today was Wednesday. "I don't think I'm going to Etoiles anymore."

"What?" Clare exclaimed, but MC said nothing.

"I told Rick I'm not going to the ball, either."

"Not going?" Clare wailed.

"After everything that's happened—Mom and Joe Riley, and now Marlon and Natalie—I just can't go. I can't pretend not to see what it stands for."

"But it's just a dance," MC said.

"It's not!" Kari didn't think she could explain it. It wasn't the politics of it. Maybe it was for Shawna, but that's not what it was for her. It was the way of life, Ma Lila's way of life, that she didn't want. The thought of going to Etoile Club parties fifty years after high school was like someone placing his hands around her throat and squeezing tight.

MC drove past Shawna's house and Kari looked at it for as long as she could. She remembered venturing onto the property, wanting to look into the window, see the kind of life Shawna led. She remembered breaking the window with the rock and running away, only, to her utter humiliation, to get caught. It still made her cringe, thinking about what she did. I should call Shawna after school, she thought, to find out what happened to Natalie.

Looking down at her hands, she saw Rick's promise ring on her finger. She hardly ever took it off; it had been almost like a part of her body. But it wasn't a part of her body. She twisted it off her finger. I was a jerk to Rick yesterday, she thought. But she couldn't wear his ring anymore.

MC parked in Kari's driveway. In the backseat, Clare still sniffled. Kari opened the door and used the crutches to pull herself to her feet, then turned to look into the car. She felt like she should say something, tell them they were still her best friends; she just needed some time to herself. But when Kari opened her mouth, all that came out was "Thanks for the ride."

"Sure," MC said, but Clare said nothing as she climbed into the front seat.

"I'll call you later," Kari said tentatively.

MC seemed to understand, even if Clare sulked at the floor. "Talk to you later."

Kari hobbled inside on her crutches where, unfortunately, Ma Lila sat in the living room.

"Kari!" She sounded surprised to see her. "What are you doing home so early?"

"My ankle hurt." Kari laid her crutches by the door and limped to the kitchen. The crutches chafed the undersides of her arms.

Ma Lila followed her into the kitchen. "I'll make you some lunch."

"Thanks," Kari said. "Can you call the attendance office for me?"

Ma Lila nodded slightly as she opened the refrigerator. Kari sat at the table. So far, she had managed to avoid Ma Lila completely. She was certain Ma Lila knew at least a little about her trip to Tennessee, and she braced herself for Ma Lila's inevitable questions.

Ma Lila soon brought a bowl of soup and a grilled cheese sandwich to the table and, to Kari's discomfort, sat down with her.

Kari took a bite of her sandwich but as she chewed it, she realized she wasn't hungry. She set it down and began stirring her soup idly, listening to the clock ticking over the counter.

"Where's Mom?" she said to break the silence.

"She went somewhere to do something," Ma Lila said. "I never know for sure what's going on with your mother."

"Neither do I," Kari said, then blushed, surprised she had said it.

Ma Lila didn't seem to notice. "So have you made your plans for prom this Saturday? I was just talking to Justine Jaenke and she said she's hosting the Etoile brunch on Sunday. And then all the barbecues and socials next week—"

Kari set down her soup spoon. All of the pre-ball events had sounded like so much fun not too long ago. Now they sounded imaginary, like an idle daydream. She looked Ma Lila in the face. "I'm not going, Ma Lila. I'm not going to any of it."

Ma Lila's hands went to her pearl necklace. "What do you mean you're not going?"

"I'm not going."

Ma Lila twisted the pearls in her hand like she was grasping them for dear life. Her mouth hung open in disbelief. "But what about Clare and MC and Rick? What about Rick?"

"They already know."

"What is the meaning of all this, young lady!" Ma Lila snapped. It was a tone of voice Kari hadn't heard from Ma Lila since she was a little girl, in trouble for misbehaving.

"I—" Kari shut her mouth and stirred her soup. She had no idea what to say to Ma Lila.

"Are you letting other people get to you, listening to those people who say the ball shouldn't happen?" Ma Lila sounded really angry.

Kari wondered what people she was talking about. Was this Ma Lila's way of talking about Shawna? "That's not it."

"It has to be it!" Ma Lila exclaimed. "What else can it be? You were so excited about the ball, your dress is hanging upstairs in your closet."

"Ma Lila—" Kari took a deep breath, wondering if there was any way to make Ma Lila understand. "It's not for me, okay? The Spring Ball's just not for me."

Ma Lila stood up, near tears. "I don't understand you young people! I just don't understand you at all!" She fled from the kitchen.

I guess that's true, thought Kari with a sigh.

{ chapter *thirty-one* }

FTER FIRST PERIOD, SHAWNA found a note taped to her locker: *Call me after school—M*. After that, she avoided the locker the rest of the day so she wouldn't run into Sephora. It still bothered her, the way Sephora felt about Natalie. Maybe Sephora was looking at the big picture. Maybe lots of black boys got beat up, or worse, for dating white girls. But how was anything going to change if everyone kept holding on to the past?

She was on her way outside at the end of the day when she heard someone call, "Hey, Shawna."

A tall blond guy was coming toward her. There was something vaguely familiar about him, but it wasn't until he was standing in front of her that Shawna realized he was Kari's boyfriend. He stood with his head lowered and his hands stuffed into the pockets of his shorts.

Shawna felt herself growing wary. "What's going on?"

"Kari broke up with me yesterday."

"Um—" Was he blaming her? "Sorry."

He sank onto the floor, leaning against a bank of lockers. Shawna hesitated, then sat down with him. "I don't get it. I don't know what I did."

"I'm sure it's not you—" But Shawna had no idea what it was. She tried to think of something specific Kari had said about her boyfriend, but she couldn't come up with anything.

"Things've been different ever since she got to know you." If he was angry, it didn't show. He stared out into space.

"What do you mean?"

"At first I thought you were putting ideas into her head."

"Don't you think she has her own ideas in her own head?"

His face reddened. "I didn't mean it like that. I saw her friend MC after lunch and MC said she took Kari home. And she said Kari's quitting Etoiles."

Shawna nodded, unsurprised.

He turned to face her. "She talk about any of this with you?"

"No. Yesterday was kind of a—weird day for us."

"Y'all went somewhere."

"You know, you'd be better off talking to Kari about this." Shawna scooted a few inches away from him.

"She won't talk to me." He didn't sound angry. He took in a deep breath and let it out slowly, his head drooping forward.

Shawna didn't know what to say. "Um, what do you think I can do?"

The tips of his ears were bright red. "I don't know."

He really cared about Kari; Shawna saw that much. "I'll talk to her if you want me to—"

He looked up quickly, like he wasn't expecting her to say that. "You'd do that?"

"I don't know if it'll help, but I can try."

He smiled a little, embarrassed-looking. "Thanks."

Shawna giggled and brought a hand to her mouth to hide it.

"What?"

"It's just weird to think of me talking to Kari for you," she said, "knowing you probably don't think all that much of me."

He scratched the side of his head. "All I know about you is what Troy tells me. I'll say I don't get you. What you're all about."

"You don't know me."

"You're right, I don't." His blush deepened. "It's gotten all around, what happened to Natalie. And I know you're friends with Marlon."

Shawna nodded.

"I dunno—some folks are saying she got what she deserved, you know?" He wouldn't look at her when he said that.

"Do you know what people are saying about Marlon?" Shawna's voice cracked and she cleared her throat.

"There's been some talk," he mumbled. He crossed his arms tightly over his chest.

"Is it bad?" Shawna's throat felt dry.

"It's just talk." He sounded as embarrassed as he looked. "That's all."

Shawna stood up. "I'll talk to Kari for you."

"Thanks," he said, and she knew he meant it. "See you around."

"See you around," Shawna echoed.

Shawna replayed the conversation in her head as she drove home. She had a feeling he didn't like her and that she made him uncomfortable. But he trusted her and, she thought, probably respected her, too. So now I'm supposed to say something to Kari on his behalf, she thought. What could she say? I'll just tell her he loves her, she told herself. Maybe it would mean something, coming from her.

The house was quiet. Dad wasn't home, and neither was Grandma Rory. Immediately, Shawna went to the phone and dialed Marlon's number. He answered on the first ring.

"It's me," Shawna said. "How's Natalie?"

"All right. I just got back from her house not too long ago."

"I got your note—"

"Well, she wanted to see you after school today."

"See me?"

"Yeah. She wants to talk to you."

Shawna didn't know what to think. "Okay."

"I'll come get you," Marlon said. "I'll be there soon."

As soon as she hung up, the phone rang again.

"Shawna?" The voice was tentative but Shawna recognized it immediately.

"Kari," she said. "What's going on?"

"I just wanted to know if you knew anything about Natalie."

"She's okay. I guess she wants to talk to me."

"Oh."

"Listen, why don't you come with me to see Natalie?"

There was a pause before Kari spoke. "All right. I'd like that."

"We'll be there soon to pick you up."

Shawna hung up and waited on the front porch for Marlon. When he pulled into her driveway, she hopped into the front seat. "We're going to pick up Kari Lang, okay?"

Marlon looked surprised, but he nodded.

"It's hard, isn't it?" she said. "All this with Natalie—"

"Yeah—" He kept his eyes on the road.

"But it's worth it, right?"

He nodded.

It stung a little, getting his answer.

She directed him to Kari's house, where Kari waited for them in the driveway. She hobbled out to the car, limping badly, and Shawna got into the backseat to make room for her.

"Kari, Marlon, do you know each other?" she said.

They looked at each other and sort of smiled.

"I'm sorry about what happened to Natalie," she said.

"So'm I," Marlon said. He glanced at her ankle. "What happened to you?"

"I fell yesterday."

They were silent as Marlon drove out toward the old sawmill. The closer they got to the sawmill, the smaller and more unkempt the houses got. He parked in front of a brick house on a corner with a brown and matted-looking front yard. Hadn't Marlon said something once about Natalie not having much money? Marlon helped Kari out of the car, and she leaned against him as they made their way up the steps to the door.

Marlon knocked, then pushed the front door open. "Natalie?" he called inside. "No one else is home," he said to Kari and Shawna.

They entered a dank hallway with a crooked banister going up a steep flight of stairs.

"Natalie's room's on this floor," Marlon said as Kari eyed the stairs. The floorboards squeaked as they walked over them.

"I guess Natalie's mom works at a carpet mill in Dalton,"

Kari whispered to Shawna. "They knew all about it in Etoiles."

"Did it matter?" Shawna whispered back.

"No, because she's so pretty. She was on the cover of some magazine last year."

"I'm not surprised."

Marlon opened the door onto a darkened room in the back of the house. The room was long and narrow, with hardly any standing room between the twin bed and the desk pushed against opposite walls. The walls were stark white and undecorated. Natalie sat on a chair looking out the window.

"Natalie?" Marlon almost whispered.

Natalie looked up and smiled, like she was grateful to see him. It made Shawna wince, seeing the dark scabs stretch around Natalie's mouth. The bruises at her eyes looked painful as well. When Natalie saw Shawna, her eyes brightened, but when she saw Kari, the smile faded and she looked nervous.

All three of them sat on the bed. Shawna half expected Natalie to get up and throw her arms around Marlon. She didn't. She remained on the chair, drawing her legs underneath her.

"How do you feel?" Shawna asked.

Natalie was still looking at Kari. "Okay. I didn't know you guys were friends."

"Our parents were friends when they were at Dessina," Kari said.

Natalie nodded, still uncomfortable-looking. "I guess all the Etoiles hate me now."

Kari shrugged. "I don't know what they think. I quit."

Natalie looked surprised. "You quit?"

"It's not my thing."

"Not mine, either. When—what's-her-name, Kessler?

When she told me about this club, I thought I'd make a whole bunch of friends that way. It's hard to make friends, being new. But now—" She turned to look out the window.

Shawna couldn't help but stare at her. Yes, Natalie was beautiful in the way girls in magazines were beautiful. She had the kind of face that would make you think, a girl like that would never have any problems. She would sail through her life without a trial, just for looking like she did. She glanced at Marlon, then back to Natalie. Was the whole forbidden fruit thing a part of it, like Dad said? But that couldn't be all. Natalie was a pariah now with the popular white kids and with the black kids, too. But then, looking at Marlon, seeing how handsome he was, she could almost get it, why those girls beat up Natalie. Almost.

"I thought you might hate me, too," Natalie said to Shawna.

Shawna was surprised. "Me, hate you?"

"You just looked so shocked when you first met me, and sometimes when I saw you in the hallways, you'd look at me like I'm dirt. And then after those girls beat me up—"

"I don't want to see anyone get hurt!" Shawna snapped.

Natalie lowered her eyes. "No, that's not what I meant. I'm sorry."

Shawna didn't answer.

"It's just that sometimes I feel like I've made a mess of things here. Sometimes I think I should go back to Ohio."

"I felt like that too sometimes," Shawna said.

Natalie looked like she didn't know what to say to that, so she turned to Kari. "Are you going to the ball?"

Kari shook her head. "What about you and Marlon?"

Natalie and Marlon looked at each other; then Natalie shook her head, too. "I think we already made our point."

"Besides, they don't want us at that ball any more than we want to be there," Marlon said. "I think we'll skip the prom, too."

"So we're all staying away?" Shawna said. "We could have our own prom. Well, you all could. I'm the fifth wheel around here."

"No, you're not," Kari mumbled.

"I saw your boyfriend today," Shawna said.

"You saw Rick?"

"He seemed really upset."

Kari frowned. "Did he say something to you?"

"What do you mean?"

"You know, say any of this is your fault? Because if he did—"

"It wasn't like that. He just seemed really hurt."

Kari looked away quickly, like her eyes had filled with tears and she didn't want anyone to see. "I was mean to him."

"Do you still love him?" Shawna asked.

Kari shrugged, then sniffled. "I don't know."

"Maybe you just need some time to yourself," Natalie offered.

Kari sniffled again, swiping a hand under her nose. "I guess so."

Shawna glanced at Marlon, who was looking around the room like he wasn't paying attention. He seemed nervous, like he had unintentionally crashed a girls-only party. "Hey, Marlon," Shawna said to get his attention.

"So y'all want to plan something for prom night?" he asked.

Natalie sat up and leaned toward Marlon. "No, let's throw a party the week after. We'll have it on the night of the Spring Ball. It'll be the Anti-Ball."

Kari giggled. "So we can all dress like General Sherman instead of General Lee?"

Marlon laughed, too. "We don't have to go that far."

"We can start a tradition!" Natalie sounded excited. "Who knows? Next year maybe our party'll be the place to be, instead of the Old South Ball."

Next year. The thought was dull and heavy in Shawna's mind. Could she stand another year at Dessina High? Another year of being stared at, told she talked funny, told she had the wrong opinions about everything? Kessler was graduating, but she'd still have Troy to clash with next year over the newspaper. But what was the alternative? Lakeview Country Day School and uniforms? Mom's big house, empty most of the time because Mom worked so much?

Shawna looked around Natalie's tiny room, at Kari and Marlon and Natalie, who were talking about the party. She remembered that night in Tennessee, the way she had opened up to Kari, told her about Jordan. Kari had simply listened without judgment, without thinking Shawna was stuck up or foolish for being in love with a coward. Looking at Kari now, there was so much Shawna wanted to say. A week ago, Shawna would have thought Kari would be the last person in Dessina she could have something in common with. But the trip to Tennessee was just the beginning. They could figure it out together: where each of them was going, what each wanted from her life. As for Marlon, her friendship meant as much to him as his meant to her; she knew that. She could give Natalie a chance, get to know her. And even if Sephora and Tashi saw the world differently than she did, they could still be friends, too.

How could I possibly leave this place? Shawna thought. But then she remembered Mom, how she would be spending the summer at Mom's house. Shawna imagined Mom was hoping she would hate Dessina and that she'd want to come back to Denver. Mom would be disappointed to hear that Shawna would spend next year in Dessina. But home for Shawna was going to be here with Dad, in the house Dad and Grandma Rory both grew up in. Maybe Dad wasn't just running home to Mommy the way her mother said he was after the divorce. Maybe he came back here to look his past in the face, to reevaluate what he wanted from his life. And that's what I'm doing, too, Shawna thought. She and Kari together.

"Hey, Shawna, you with us?" Marlon asked.

Shawna shook her head quickly. "What?"

"You just looked like you were somewhere else."

"I was just thinking about next year."

"What about it?" Natalie asked.

"Well, I'm going to stay with my mom this summer."

Kari looked disappointed. "All summer?"

"And I know Mom really wants me to come back and live with her."

"What are you gonna do?" Marlon asked.

Shawna didn't even have to think about it. "I'm coming back here. I'm coming back here and it's going to be better next year."

{ chapter *thirty-two* }

MARLON DROPPED HER OFF, getting out to walk her up to her front door. Kari tried to remember anything Rick or Troy had ever said about him. They had always liked him, hadn't they? She wondered what they thought of him now.

Daddy was home, watching the evening news. For a moment, Kari stood in the doorway, watching him. Her eyes traced his curly red hair, his red eyebrows, his good-natured face. What did Mom see in Daddy? She rarely saw them together now because they worked such different schedules. At Sunday dinners, Mom and Daddy got along like two people who'd known each other so long they didn't have to explain much to the other. They didn't seem to be madly in love, but they seemed satisfied.

Daddy saw her standing in the doorway. "Cherry!" he said, but he didn't open his arms wide. Instead, he patted the sofa and Kari sat beside him.

How much did he know about everything? Did he know that she told Mom she hated her? Kari felt bad now, thinking about that. But she knew she couldn't take it back, once she had said it. Now she didn't know what to say at all.

"It's been a rough week," he said.

"Yeah."

"Your mother told me all about it."

"I'm quitting Etoiles."

Daddy didn't look surprised, but he didn't say anything about it.

"I'm not going to the ball with Rick, either. Ma Lila's real upset about it."

"I reckon she would be."

"I just don't think it's my thing."

"Nobody said it had to be your thing."

"I'm just so mixed up about everything." Kari sighed. "When I thought Mom had a baby with Joe Riley, I got so excited!" She stopped, looking closely at Daddy for a reaction.

He gave none she could read. "From what I hear, you girls were pretty upset."

"It's just that we got our hopes up."

"What did you really want from all this?"

Kari thought for a long time. Was it really a sibling she wanted, or was it something more than that? "I guess I really just wanted to be friends with Shawna."

"And did you get what you wanted?"

Kari smiled. "Yeah, I guess I did."

He put an arm around her shoulder and squeezed her tight. "I'm glad."

But Kari wasn't all the way satisfied. "Daddy? Do you love Mom?"

"Of course I love your mother," he said. "People don't have to be exactly alike to love each other. But we both want the same things from life, and we both got you."

"It's just that Mom—" Kari didn't know what to say.

"You and your mother are different kinds, too. Doesn't mean you don't love each other."

"I guess so. I just wish I—knew myself better."

Daddy shrugged. "If you got yourself all figured out at the age of sixteen, what the hell're you gonna do with the rest of your life?"

Kari leaned against Daddy's shoulder.

The doorbell rang. "I'll get that." He left the room and moments later, MC and Clare came in together.

"Kari—" Clare sat beside her and grasped her hand. "We just got back from Etoiles and everybody misses you. Even Jolie and Kessler. They said they're gonna come over and talk to you to see if there's anything they can do." She paused. "Kari, what's happened?"

MC stood in the doorway, watching.

"We wanted to talk to you about the ball," Clare said. "We planned it all out, remember? Renting a limo—"

"You know what?" Kari said. "I just got back from seeing Natalie Curran."

"How is she?" asked MC.

"She's gonna be okay. But she and Marlon, they're not going to prom or the ball."

"Thank goodness—" Clare muttered.

Kari looked up sharply.

"Well, you don't know what'll happen if they show up!" Clare exclaimed. "Look what happened to Natalie already!"

"They've already made their point," MC put in.

"Marlon and Natalie are gonna have a party the day of the ball," Kari said. "If y'all wanna come—"

Clare stood up, furious. "You're just being stuck up! Are you too good for us now, too good for the ball?"

Kari looked over at MC, who still stood in the doorway. Did MC understand?

"Kari," MC said. "Me and Jake'll stop by the party you're having."

Kari smiled. "Thanks." She looked at Clare, who still looked angry.

"Whatever. I guess Tim and I'll come for a little while, too," Clare muttered.

"I'm glad," Kari said.

Clare still looked angry. "I feel like you want me to give up Etoiles, too. And I'm mad at you for that."

Kari took a deep breath. "I don't want you to do anything like that. I know you like Etoiles. It's just not for me anymore."

Clare still looked upset.

"We don't all have to do the same things to be best friends," Kari said. "We don't have to all be alike."

"But what are you like now?" Clare asked.

"I don't know, exactly," Kari said. "Something in me's really changed. I don't know."

"I've been thinking about everything that's happened to you." MC came to sit on the other side of Kari, but she didn't grasp her hand like Clare did.

"What do you think of it all?" Kari asked.

MC shook her head slowly. "I don't know. I don't know what I'd do if anything like that happened to me."

"Really?" Kari was surprised to hear that. MC always seemed to know the right thing to do, the right thing to say.

That's what made her so different from everybody else Kari knew.

"Everything you did with Shawna, it all seems so, I don't know, important," MC went on. "It's the kind of thing you'll remember when you've forgotten everything else about high school."

"I guess so." Kari looked from MC to Clare, sitting on either side of her. Clare continued to sulk, folding her arms over her chest. She had known Clare and MC since preschool; she could hardly remember not knowing them. MC, Kari, and Clare: It had always been the three of them, doing everything together. But now she felt like Shawna, who'd only known her for a short time, knew more about her than MC and Clare did. Shawna understood her better. What would happen now with MC and Clare? Would they slowly drift apart, go their separate ways? The thought was sad and scary at the same time.

"I've got some homework to do," MC said, standing up. "We'd better go, Clare."

Clare got up and walked to the doorway. MC turned and pressed her hand into Kari's for a moment.

"I'll see you tomorrow," MC said.

Kari nodded.

"Before school. You want me to pick you up, right?" MC looked anxious, like she wasn't sure what Kari's answer would be.

Kari smiled, seeing MC so worried. Maybe things would change between them, maybe they wouldn't do everything together anymore, but Kari knew they would always be friends. "I'll see you tomorrow morning," she said.

MC smiled. Clare left the room without looking back.

When they were gone, Kari lay back on the couch with her hands under her head. She could still hear Clare asking her what she was like now. Maybe Daddy was right; maybe it didn't matter if she didn't have herself all figured out yet. Or maybe I'm not really changing, she told herself. Maybe she'd been different all along and never knew it, drifting along by doing what everybody else did.

"Kari?"

Kari looked up to see Mom standing in the doorway. Her shoulders stiffened as she sat up.

Mom came to sit on the couch and Kari eyed her suspiciously. But Mom didn't look angry or upset. Nothing on her face showed that she was mad at Kari for saying she hated her.

"What do you want?" Kari sounded colder than she meant to.

Mom's eyes went to Kari's ankle. "You should elevate it when you're sitting down."

Kari shrugged. "It doesn't hurt too bad."

"Your grandmother tells me you're not going to the Spring Ball," Mom said.

"She upset?"

"I think sometimes she tries to relive her life through you."

"I can't go," Kari said. "I just can't."

Mom nodded, like she understood.

"Besides, I've got other plans now."

Mom looked interested. "Oh?"

"Me and Shawna, and Marlon and Natalie." Kari paused. "Do you know about Marlon and Natalie?"

"Tell me about them."

"Well, it's something like you and Joe Riley," Kari said. "Except that they wrote an article in the newspaper, telling everybody how they feel."

"And how did that go over at Dessina High?"

"About like you'd expect."

"So your plans, they're with Shawna and this couple—"

"We're having an Anti-Ball," Kari said. "We're gonna invite a bunch of people. Clare and MC, they said they'd come by before they go to the ball."

Mom smiled. "Your party sounds like a good idea."

Kari nodded. She still felt like she should apologize to Mom for saying she hated her. "Mom?" Kari hesitated. She didn't know quite what to say.

Mom reached around her neck and moments later, she was holding the necklace she'd had made from Joe Riley's arrowhead.

"I always meant to learn more about this." Mom held the gold chain so that the arrowhead swayed like a pendulum. "Find out more about the hunting ground where Joe found it."

"You never did?"

Mom shook her head. "I even forgot I had it. I put it away in a jewelry box and it stayed there for years. But one day, I was looking for a pair of earrings and I came across it." She gathered the necklace in her hand. The chain was barely visible, making Kari wonder how something so fine could carry a pendant so heavy-looking.

But when Mom placed the necklace in Kari's hand, Kari saw that the arrowhead wasn't heavy at all. The arrowhead was spade-shaped more than triangular. It was a pale pink, marbled through with grayish glints. She wondered what type of rock it was made from. Kari ran her fingers over the rough, notched edges.

Kari held it out to Mom, but Mom shook her head. "It's yours now," she said.

"Why are you giving this to me?"

"You keep it."

Kari let the chain spill through her fingers. She could barely feel its weight against her hand. "But I don't know what it means."

Mom looked down at the arrowhead. She seemed to be tracing its outline with her eyes. "It can mean whatever you want it to mean."

Kari felt like Mom was trying to tell her something, but she didn't know what it was.

"Joe and I weren't looking for anything when we went on that hike up in Amicalola," Mom said. "I remember it started to rain when we were halfway up the trail. A really light, cool rain. We sat under a tree to rest a while and all we could hear was the rain drizzling on the leaves. Neither one of us said anything. It was like we didn't want to disturb the quiet. It was such a grand feeling, just sitting there with Joe, listening to the falling rain. We never really talked about it, but I think we were both feeling the same thing. That we were part of something bigger than we could have ever imagined."

Kari had never seen Mom look like this, so peaceful and yet so sad at the same time. It made her feel strange inside. Strange and exhilarated. "Tell me more about it," she said.

"Joe was resting his hands on the ground and then he felt something. I saw him pick up something muddy-looking and smooth it off. I thought it was just a rock at first, even though it didn't really look like the kind of rock you normally see up there. Joe looked at it carefully, ran his hands over it. And then he told me it was an arrowhead."

"How did he know?"

"He showed me the notches on the side, showed me how the face had been smoothed over. And it made me realize, people have been coming here for a long, long time. Of course we all know that people have lived in those mountains for centuries. But sometimes, we get so caught up in our own lives that we forget we're a part of something bigger."

Kari looked down at the arrowhead, running her thumb over its face. "That's what I feel," she said. "There's so much more to life than what goes on at Dessina High School."

Mom smiled. "And that's why you were so curious about Shawna Riley?"

Kari nodded. Mom really did understand.

"And that's why you wanted to have something you could share between you?" Mom said. "A brother or a sister?"

Kari winced and tears filled her eyes. It still hurt, thinking about Tennessee.

But Mom looked sad, too. "I'm sorry you were so disappointed."

Kari shrugged and wiped her eyes quickly. What could she say to that?

Mom's hand went to Kari's shoulder and it lingered there. "Joe and I may not have given you girls a sibling, but you have something else, right?"

Kari wasn't sure what Mom meant. She wasn't talking about the necklace, Kari knew that. And Kari didn't think she was talking about friendship, either. Daddy was right; Kari did want to be friends with Shawna all along. But something else had happened when Kari and Shawna went to Tennessee together. She remembered riding in Shawna's car on their way to Knoxville, heading uphill on Old Dessina Road with the setting sun in front of them. And she remembered feeling for the first time what it meant to do something on her own, take charge of her own life, find out what she really wanted.

Mom had tears in her eyes. "You girls did something really special."

"What do you mean?" Kari whispered.

Mom's arm went around her, and Kari felt the warmth of Mom's cheek pressed against hers. "You brought two old friends together again."

"I guess we did, didn't we." Kari wiped her face and watched Mom reach up to wipe hers.

Kari propped her hurt ankle on the coffee table and slowly rotated it, feeling the pain stinging her lower leg. What was it about running that she liked so much? The feeling of wind on her face. Speed and motion. Even that achy tiredness that came after, when she would sink onto the couch and shut her eyes, exhausted but content. But it was more than that, now that she thought about it. Running was the only time in which the world was completely hers, without Ma Lila or the Etoiles or Rick leaning over her, telling her what kind of girl she should be. Her senses seemed to sharpen whenever she was out running. She could practically feel the world taking shape around her.

Kari turned to Mom and saw Mom smiling back at her. Maybe Mom was never really aloof in the way Kari had always thought. Mom was the only woman in Kari's life who gave her the space to figure out what she wanted for herself. Mom would never tell her how to dress, how to act, or how to be. Mom would accept her for whoever and whatever she was.

"You know what I wish I could do right now?" Kari said as she and Mom settled back on the couch.

"Tell me."

"Go on a nice long jog."

"It'll be a couple of weeks before you can do anything like that," Mom said.

Kari imagined herself climbing Old Dessina Road and then continuing on past the school, out where the road wound through open country, snaking its way upward toward Chattanooga. She would focus completely on the road in front of her, where it would take her next instead of where she had already been.

"As soon as my ankle gets better," Kari said, "I'm gonna start running again."